From the bestselling authors of *Atlantis* and *Silver!*

Navy SEAL Dane Maddock leads a team of operatives in a race against Russian Spetznaz agents to find a lost nuclear submarine and recover a threat known only as Romanov's Bane, but the frozen wasteland of Wrangel Island is home to more than enemy soldiers. Soon, Dane and Bones find themselves face-to-face with dangers thought long extinct. Join them as they seek to foil a madman's deadly plot in the action-packed thriller, *Dead Ice*.

Praise for Dead Ice

"Another rip-roaring thrill ride of an adventure for Dane and Bones! Thriller fans won't want to miss!" –Joseph Nassise, international bestselling author of *The Templar Chronicles*.

"Call in sick tomorrow, it's going to be a late night! Shades of Jurassic Park set against a Russian special forces backdrop with old friends Dane and Bones at it again--Dead Ice is dead on!" -Rick Chesler, author of *Solar Island* and *Wired Kingdom*

Praise for the Dane Maddock Adventures

"Dane and Bones.... Together they're unstoppable. Rip roaring action from start to finish. Wit and humor throughout. Just one question – how soon until the next one? Because I can't wait." - Graham Brown, author of *Shadows of the Midnight Sun*

"Packs in the fist fights, cipher cracking and ancient secrets that all action adventure lovers will enjoy."- J.F. Penn, author of the *ARKANE* thrillers

A DANE AND BONES ORIGINS STORY

DAVID WOOD
STEVEN SAVILE

Gryphonwood

Gryphonwood Press

DEAD ICE- A DANE AND BONES ORIGINS
STORY.

Published by Gryphonwood Press
www.gryphonwoodpress.com

Cover by Scott Macumber
Edited by Michael Dunne

ISBN-10: 1940095190
ISBN-13: 978-1-940095-19-6

Printed in the United States of America
First printing: July, 2014

Books by David Wood

The Dane Maddock Adventures
Dourado
Cibola
Quest
Icefall
Buccaneer
Atlantis

Dane and Bones Origins
Freedom (with Sean Sweeney)
Hell Ship (with Sean Ellis)
Splashdown (with Rick Chesler)
Dead Ice (with Steven Savile)
Liberty (with Edward G. Talbot- forthcoming)

Stand-Alone Works
Into the Woods (with David S. Wood)
Callsign: Queen (with Jeremy Robinson)
Dark Rite (with Alan Baxter)
The Zombie-Driven Life

The Dunn Kelly Mysteries
You Suck
Bite Me (forthcoming)

Writing as David Debord
The Silver Serpent
Keeper of the Mists
The Gates of Iron (forthcoming)
The Impostor Prince (with Ryan A. Span-forthcoming)

Books by Steven Savile

The Ogmios Series
Solomon's Seal
Wargod
Lucifer's Machine
Silver

Other Works
Black Chalice
Each Ember's Ghost
Sign of Glaaki
Risen 2: Dark Waters

And many more…

PROLOGUE

Karl Gustavovich Fabergé did not look up from his work when, unheralded, Nikolai bustled through the door. He raised one hand, forestalling further interruption.

"Go outside, close the door, and knock." Fabergé remained calm and kept his eyes on his work as he gave these instructions. His work required focus and attention to detail, and he could not allow the temerity of a foolish assistant to put him out of sorts.

"Master, someone is here to see you."

Now Fabergé looked up. Nikolai's interruption had been out of character, but for the young man to ignore his command, that was something else entirely. Furthermore, there was a tremor in Nikolai's voice, and a breathy quality to his voice that was so unlike him.

Fabergé looked his assistant up and down. Nikolai's skin was the color of new-fallen snow, and perspiration ran in rivulets down his cheeks. What had put him out of sorts? Fabergé made a placating gesture.

"Calm yourself and explain."

"Master, you have a visitor. He says he has plans for an egg…"

"Plans for an egg?" Now Fabergé's ire rose. "I have always been free to make every egg as I choose. The royal family wishes it so. Whoever this visitor is, tell him to go away. I have no time for such foolishness."

He turned back to his work, thinking the matter at an end, but Nikolai hurried to his side and reached out a trembling hand, nearly touching Fabergé's arm.

"Master, please. This is not a man to be turned away." His voice had fallen to a hoarse whisper, and he kept glancing at the door, as if whoever waited outside might enter at any time.

Fabergé took three deep breaths, restoring himself to his usual calm. "Very well. Did he bring these plans with him?"

Nikolai nodded.

"Take his name and tell him to leave them with you and I will review them. If I wish to make this egg for him, I will contact him."

"I fear that will not be possible." The voice that came from the direction of the doorway put Fabergé in mind of a serpent, due both to its hypnotic quality and the faint hiss that underscored his last word.

The man that stepped into the room seemed impossibly tall. His lean body and long face, hair, and beard only served to exaggerate his height. His intense eyes burned into Fabergé, freezing him in place.

"Leave us," the man said to Nikolai, who scurried out the door, giving the stranger a wide berth as they passed.

Even if there had not been two uniformed, armed men standing just outside the doorway, Fabergé would have been powerless to protest this intruder giving orders to his staff. The tall man's aura was too strong. It was not charisma, exactly, but something like...

...witchcraft.

Perhaps the stories were true.

Fabergé tried to speak, but found his mouth dry as a desert.

"Forgive me for the intrusion. I know it is the height of discourtesy, but I fear my business cannot wait." The man was all courtesy now, though condescension twinkled in his eyes.

Nevertheless, the ice now broken, Fabergé managed to speak.

"How may I be of service to you?"

"As your man told you, I need you to craft an egg. A special egg." The words hung in the air as he reached inside his coat and produced a leather cylinder from which he extracted a roll of papers."

Fabergé noted a slight tremor to the man's hand as he passed the plans over to him. He spread the plans out on a table and looked them over. They were all wrong. A note in the margin, written in a spider hand, specified a thickness that would make the egg far too fragile. And the other details…

"I realize the design is not consistent with the other eggs which you have so expertly made, but it will serve my purpose."

"Purpose? There is no purpose to the eggs beyond the artistic. To what use could you possibly put this?" He tapped the plans with one slender finger.

The smile spreading across the man's face did not reach his eyes.

"One which could change the world."

ONE

"Стой!"

The man didn't break his stride, didn't glance back at those chasing him, yelling at him to stop. He ran for his life. Moonlight glinted on the rain soaked street, only to be trampled and splashed by expensive Italian leather shoes designed for anything but running, and metal tipped boots that clattered and echoed between the tenements of a harsh city.

"Стой!" Louder this time. Demanding. Stop! Soon they'd shoot.

He reached a narrow redbrick alleyway, ducked into it and kept running. He knew these streets and back alleys, not well, but well enough not to be herded into a dead end. The buildings were in a state of decay far worse than a few broken streetlights suggested. The rot lay deep and pervasive, and the fetid odor of urine and rotting garbage hung in the air. Back home they'd have been condemned and torn down. Here they were home to the poor and used as a mask to hide the horrors of the regime. He had to use it to his advantage if he was going to make it to the rendezvous in time. It was vital that the information he was carrying reached the right hands. After that nothing else mattered. He would have done his job. He'd always known the risks.

He almost lost his footing as he turned left then right, ducking under a sagging washing line strung with grime stained vests and underwear that surely hadn't been washed before being hung out. The double-back bought him a few precious seconds while he was out of sight, then he hit the open space of the unlit courtyard before a towering block of apartments. He tipped over a few trash cans, spilling garbage across the narrow path, hoping to slow the pursuit. To his left he saw a rusty wrought-iron gate that hung open on a shadowy doorway. Beyond it, barely visible, the first couple of stone steps leading up. He ran for them, climbing the stairs three and four steps at a time, then rushed along a walkway that overlooked the courtyard. He looked down. He shouldn't have looked down. The first of the men hunting him stumbled into one of the overturned cans trying to avoid the garbage strewn across the path. His curse barely carried as far as the walkway. The tactic maybe bought him half a second.

He had to keep moving. There had to be a way out of this rat hole.

He checked the grime crusted windows as he ran past the apartments. He didn't know exactly where he was going. A little divine intervention would be gratefully accepted. One door along here, he hoped, would get them off his trail. The first two were lit by dim lamps and the muted glow of television sets; tiny sets in tiny rooms and yet the people watching them did not know anything bigger or better. Those tiny sets were as close to luxury as they'd ever come. They had been raised good Communists, content with their lot, and did not deserve the fate he could bring to their door. Forcing his way into any one of those homes would ruin their lives. He didn't want to do that to them.

But if he had to, he would.

At the far end of the walkway he saw what he was looking for.

Even with the bare bulb above shattered, the limited light was enough to see that the door had been forced open. Jags of splintered wood around the frame betrayed the fact the apartment had been broken into despite the fact the door had been pushed back in to place to disguise the invasion. It was one of many, he was sure. Not the best for his purpose, but the closest. It would do.

The echo of boots in the concrete stairwell meant it

was now or never.

He didn't like never.

He pushed in through the doorway ready for the inevitable fight. The shock. The screams.

Voices came thick and fast, some startled and angry others slurred and listless; mostly men, but there were a couple of women. They screamed as he knew they would. Bodies scrambled in the dim light; some in search of clothes, snatching them up from where they had been abandoned. At least one of them was reaching for more than a discarded shoe. He charged right into the middle of the chaos, his hands held up to show that he was unarmed. Not a threat. They need to understand he wasn't a threat. He was a victim. Hopefully they *weren't* good Communists. He was banking on that slim hope.

"Помогите мне!" he said.

Help me.

He wasn't begging. He looked back over his shoulder, making it obvious that he was being chased, and knowing that these kinds of people wouldn't like the people chasing him. He'd led them, literally, into a lion's den.

One of them nodded toward a screen door—the kitchen. He stepped through it. A woman stood over the sink. She wasn't doing the dishes. She seemed to be marking out lines of coke. He stood with his back to the wall. He could see the door through a trick of perspective, from a mirror in the kitchen to a mirror in the hall.

The first man appeared in the doorway. He carried a Kalash. A Kalashnikov Automatic. A monster of a gun. It didn't help him.

The first gunshot came a heartbeat later.

A single shot followed by the crash of the gunman stumbling backward into the doorframe.

The second shot hit as he slid to the floor, leaving a smear of blood on the faded flowered wallpaper above his head.

His fingers closed on the trigger of his automatic, the pistol bucking as he unleashed a hail of bullets indiscriminately into the drug-hazed smoke filling room. If the gods came in bullet form he'd just released an entire pantheon into this small space, silencing all unbelievers.

When the bullets stopped, he was dead.

The second man wasn't so eager to die. He paused beyond the threshold, out of line-of-sight. But once the shooting stopped, he made his move, coming in fast and low. The apartment was filled with echoes and silence and the smell of death.

He watched the hunter through the mirrors as he turned over the corpses in search of his target, kicking them with his booted foot so their jaws jutted out proudly in the face of the reaper. Obviously, the target wasn't amongst the dead. There were three other rooms in the small apartment. He gestured for his companions to go right and left, checking each room off.

The woman had given up on the white lines and curled up in a ball beside the kitchen sink. Above her head, an open window waited. He could see the wrought-iron railings of a fire escape.

The metal groaned under his weight as he descended.

He moved as quickly as he could without his feet clanging on each step, knowing it was only a matter of time before they realized where he'd gone. Every second he could gain the better; every step could make a difference.

The staccato rattle of gunfire filled the air before he'd descended a single floor.

Lights went on in some of the flats. The sensible ones stayed dark. Whatever was going on had nothing to do with them; they knew better than to be nosy. Curiosity killed more than cats.

He heard the door above him swing open.

He didn't turn around to look.

He couldn't afford a moment's delay.

He stumbled as his foot reached the cracked concrete at the bottom of the stairway. His knee bent and he fought to stay upright as the clatter of pursuit sounded hot on his heels. The entire fire escape trembled beneath the weight of it. The gunman was descending fast, gaining on him. There had been three of them in the apartment, but now it sounded as though only one of them had followed him out of the window, which meant the other two had gone back out to the walkway and would work their way around to the back of the apartment block.

He ducked into the blackest of shadows, hugging close to the building.

A light went on inside one of the ground floor rooms, throwing bright light over his face for a second before he ducked back into shadow.

It was enough to give him away.

No point in trying to be quiet now.

To live he needed to run like the wind blowing through the canyons of the city. Anything else meant death. He was a rat in a maze, three ratters looking to feast on him before he found the cheese. He could only hope he knew these desolate streets better than his hunters did. He risked the briefest of glances at his watch. Ten minutes— that was all he had. If he didn't get there in time this would all have been for nothing. Dying was always a risk. It came with the territory. Failure though, failure belonged in another zip code.

He turned a corner, heading away from the ranks of tower blocks, running hard for the main road. Cars, some with only one working headlight, rumbled along the poorly lit road. Some drove so slowly, crawling along the curb, that their purpose was clear. A Saab slowed to a halt a hundred yards ahead of him. A young woman with bleached blond hair and a skirt that barely covered her goods bent down to talk to the driver. She thrust her hip out, advertising it to the other drivers as if to say, *Look what could be yours, the freshest meat your rubles can buy.* The red sequins on her skirt glittered cheaply in the streetlight. He kept running right toward them, willing the driver to move on.

She opened the passenger side door and slid inside.

She slammed the door.

He was too late. The window had closed.

She was being withdrawn.

He kept on running, willing her to see him. The car pulled away from the curb, crawling toward him. He glanced over his shoulder as the gunman came skidding around the corner.

Time's up.

Then the saw the girl's hand reach out through the open passenger side window. She'd recognized him. He had one chance as they were pulling out into traffic to make the handover. His fist closed around the secrets he'd risked his life to get out of Mother Russia. He made the drop, literally and figuratively, letting the package fall into her hand as their fingers brushed. He didn't break his stride. Maybe the gunman saw it, maybe he didn't. The Saab accelerated away.

He ducked right, relief surging through his system. He'd done it. The information in that package was worth dying for, and now it was free. The woman would get it back to her handler, and he'd get it out of the country. In silent warfare, it would be a whisper that would be heard all around the world. And it was down to him.

He had three choices. Left, right or straight ahead.

He chose left.

He chose badly.

It took him into a blind alley between apartment complexes that opened out into a courtyard for the neighboring buildings to hang their laundry and beat the dust out of heavy rugs. There was only one way out of the courtyard. Back the way he'd come.

He raised his hands above his head, knowing that he had nowhere left to run.He lowered his head. He'd made a mistake that would cost him his life.

But he hadn't failed. That was all that mattered.

He turned slowly. He looked up as the first shot was fired.

He didn't feel it.

TWO

One room looked like every other conference room in every other jurisdiction, in every other part of hell. It didn't matter which city it was in, which state, or even which country. This one was on the Coronado military base in California, but could just as easily have been in a hotel in Anchorage now that the blinds had been closed.

The people in the room waited for the briefing to start.

They didn't know why there were here, but looking around the room, seeing who had been assembled, it was obvious that it was important. At least Zara Leopov assumed everyone else was in the dark. She certainly had no idea why she had been summoned. Her position in naval intelligence didn't put her in the same room as the top brass that often. She resisted the temptation to count the pips on the uniforms around the table, afraid she'd lose count. It was readily apparent that most of the men knew each other. She was the only outsider here. They barely even spared her a second glance, assuming she was here to make the coffee. This was a testosterone-fueled world, after all.

Another uniform entered. She started to get to her feet, but the commander sitting beside her placed a hand on her shoulder and gently pushed her into her back seat. It wasn't an overtly friendly gesture. He leaned in close and whispered, "I don't know who you are, girl, or what you are doing here, but you *are* here, and you are *meant* to be here. That means you're every bit as important as the rest of the blowhards at this particular dance. As long as you're in this room, you don't stand for a superior officer. You'd be permanently on your feet."

She gave him a nervous look and saw he was smiling.

"Thank you, sir."

He nodded.

Someone dimmed the lights.

A face appeared on the screen at the front of the room. She recognized the man. It had been months since they last met. A year or more, she realized. His name was Jackson Carlisle. It was the kind of name mentioned in hushed tones throughout Naval Intelligence. She hadn't known him well, but he was one of theirs. A month ago they'd got word of his death.

From near darkness a voice began.

"As most of you already know, a US citizen, Jackson Carlisle, was shot and killed in the Russian port of Murmansk. The story the Russians have given us is that he was in the red light district and managed to get himself shot because he refused to pay a prostitute."

Leopov shook her head but said nothing, recognizing it as a better work of fiction than anything Tolstoy managed in his lifetime. She knew that Jackson wasn't that kind of guy. The picture changed. The photo of the handsome man in the prime of his life was replaced by the grey image of a face no longer touched by it.

"The body was returned to us along with his personal effects. Needless to say we were a little surprised that although no autopsy had been carried out, the bullet that killed him had been removed. While we have no evidence we suspect that it was fired from either a Kalashnikov or a Makarov. What we do know is that Carlisle was assassinated by the KGB while he was in the act of completing a mission of the utmost importance to our National Security. We lost a good man, people."

A murmur went around the room but none of them reached Leopov's ears.

She was the cuckoo in their nest.

It was the way she'd been treated since she'd joined the service. Part of it was because she was a woman, but just as much of it came down to her name. It didn't make any difference that she had been barely been able to walk when she had come to the States, or that her father had died getting his wife and daughter out of Russia. It was all about her name.

The picture on the screen changed. She felt a wave of relief. It had been hard enough to see his picture again, reminding her of how full of life he had been, but harder still to see him in death. The new image was a satellite picture of an island.

"It has taken our code breakers a while to decrypt the information he paid for with his life, and while I cannot provide all of the details at this moment, I can confirm that he provided us with the coordinates for this island in the Arctic Ocean."

Leopov recognized the coordinates, and when someone in the near darkness asked where, she had no hesitation in saying, "Russian territory." The words came tumbling from her lips before she had even realized that she was speaking out loud. She was only too aware of eyes turning in her direction to the sound of breaths being taken. "Sorry," she said to break the moment of silence that filled the room. "I..."

"Forgive me," the speaker said, preventing the embarrassment from lasting any longer than it needed to. "This is Lieutenant Leopov. She has been lent to us by Naval Intelligence."

Leopov could almost feel the dagger of ice the sound of her name thrust into the room. She felt the heat rise in her cheeks, but forced a thin-lipped smile as she nodded to those looking in her direction.

"Lieutenant Leopov has been studying satellite data about the island, which as she quite rightly says, lies within Russian territory."

The image on the large screen changed to show a closer view, and then again, zooming in frame by frame.

Leopov was familiar with these images, she had spent most the last few weeks watching the slightest changes in the pictures that came through every time the satellite passed overhead.

"I'm sorry to put you on the spot, but perhaps you could tell us what you believe this picture is showing?"

She nodded. She took a sip of water to compose herself, trying to decide what she felt she could tell the men that were gathered around the table.

"Please." The man offered his pointer to her. It was not the first time she had given a briefing, but she was coming into this blind. She'd have appreciated some kind of warning. She rose to her feet and took a deep breath as she moved to the front. She took the pointer from him.

"Wrangel Island lies in the Arctic Ocean, as I said, within Russian territory," she began. She knew that she was repeating herself, but she wanted to make sure everyone was on the same page. She couldn't just assume everyone got the implications of what she was about to say. "We have known for some time that the Russians have been using this island as an internment camp." She pointed to a couple of the buildings, indicating what she believed to be accommodation blocks, then traced the pointer along a black line that surrounded the buildings. "This is a high security perimeter fence, with lookout towers here and here," she pointed again.

"How many prisoners are held in this camp?" a voice asked.

"Maybe a thousand in these areas here," She traced the pointer along the image, picking out parts of the camp. She moved the pointer again to a separate section of the photograph. "But in this section there is only one, kept separate from the rest of the prisoners."

Now she'd got their attention.

"One? Why would they keep one man in solitary confinement?" the same voice asked, then answered his own question. "Someone who needs protection from the other inmates?"

"Perhaps the security is to keep people out rather than someone in?" another suggested.

"We are sure that this is a prisoner who stays in quarters here." She pointed again to a building the same size as one of the other accommodation blocks. We have seen him alone in what we have termed the Exercise Yard. No one else goes into that space other than those going to and from the towers."

"He gets that block to himself when the other thousand are squeezed into those dozen huts? Are you sure?"

"Absolutely," she assured the room.

"It seems a little extreme, doesn't it? Building a separate part of a prison for one man?"

"Rudolph Hess has been the only prisoner in Spandau for nearly twenty years." This observation came from the man who had been sitting next to her. "Clearly whoever this man is, we can assume he is *very* important to someone. Yet, at the same time, the Russians don't want to shout about him? Now, ask yourself this, why do you think that would that be? What makes this man so special? That seems like a very important question to me. Lieutenant Leopov?"

"As of yet we don't know."

"Yet is a very powerful word," the man noted. "It implies you will do soon."

She nodded. "We know how many people are permanently on the island and have been able to identify some of the people who have visited the island recently. At least one of them was a high ranking officer of the Red Army. We believe the two are linked in some way." When distilled to its essence she realized how little they had actually learned about the island. It felt like they had been wasting so much time to get so little tangible information.

"Thank you, Lieutenant," the man held his hand out for the return of his pointer, signaling that her part in the briefing had come to an end. Leopov handed it over, wondering if she had really told anyone anything they hadn't known. She made her way back to her seat, relieved to receive a reassuring nod from the man beside her.

"You did fine," he whispered. "And now I'm thinking that's not the only reason you've been brought here."

A frown crumpled her face, but the man said no more.

The picture changed to show another face she had seen more than once in the last month.

"General Alexei Abramovitch. This is the man we believe has visited Wrangel Island a number of times over the last few months. Forgive me if this information has been kept from you Lieutenant, but it was felt that it would be better if we restricted this information to a need to know basis until this point."

"Well, she was certainly right about it being a high ranking official in the Red Army." The man next to her sat up straight, nodding at the screen. "They don't have many fish bigger than this guy."

"Indeed," the presenter continued. "Abramovitch is a hard liner, very vocally uncomfortable with the way President Gorbachev is cozying up to the West. If he had just a little more support within the military his star would be on the rise and we'd be looking to the skies."

The reference to a nuclear assault wasn't lost on any of them.

The shadow of nuclear winter was a long one, but Leopov couldn't believe anyone thought it would actually come down to that. Mutually assured destruction? That way lay madness.

"The plot thickens. I'm guessing he wasn't taking a holiday on this little of island of theirs? Making a spot inspection to make sure that prisoners are being treated well would be a little below his pay grade, too."

"That's correct, Commander. We believe that Abramovitch has been visiting the prisoner being held in isolation." He brought up another picture before there was the chance for anyone else to ask further questions. The man was clearly used to being in control, even amongst this group of officers. Leopov suspected he might be CIA.

"The intelligence that Carlisle managed to get out of Russia related to an *Echo II* Class submarine that has managed to get itself trapped in the ice around Wrangel Island. This submarine carried something either to or from the island; something referred to as Pandora's Egg."

"And do we know what this Pandora's Egg is?" the commander asked.

"Not with any certainty, no, but we have suspicions. Or should I say concerns. Hence the perceived risk to National Security"

"No shit." The commander's language took Leopov by surprise. "So we come back to the same question we started out with: what makes this prisoner so special?"

"Unfortunately, this is where our intelligence starts to get a little hazy. We are piecing together bits of knowledge, and that means making some assumptions as we try and make sense of it."

"You mean that you're connecting the dots and hoping that your picture of a duck is right and that it shouldn't have been an elephant? From where I'm sitting, it looks as if you've jumped the gun, hauling us all in here without any real evidence to support your concerns. Frankly, I'm not even sure there is a threat that we should be concerned about."

The man didn't try and hide his anger. He was clearly seething at the commander's tone, not used to being spoken to like a child. The image behind him changed from the shot of a submarine to a grainy photograph of an old man, his shoulders hunched as he looked forward like a tortoise peering from its shell. "This is the only image of the prisoner on Wrangel Island."

"I've never seen this before," Leopov whispered to herself, loud enough for her neighbor to hear.

"So are you telling me we actually know who the prisoner is?" the commander asked.

"Not definitively. We *think* it might be this man. A second image appeared next to it like some conjurer's trick. It was the face of a much younger man, but even then clearly not in the first flush of youth. "His name is Doctor Hans Luber, stationed in the Majdanek concentration camp from nineteen forty three to forty five."

"What makes you think that this is the same man?"

"The Soviets liberated the camp just as the war was drawing to an end. Even that early in the game the Russians saw the benefit of learning the secrets that the German scientists had discovered in their experiments, even though they would never have carried them out themselves. Luber's experiments involved exposing prisoners to radioactive materials. There are rumors of other, equally unsavory practices, but they amount to little more than whispers. We know that he was stationed at Majdanek at the time of the liberation, but he disappeared off the face of the earth from that date onward."

"So the Russians shipped him back to the middle of nowhere and gave him a never-ending bunch of prisoners to experiment on?"

"So you think this place is some modern day camp?" another officer asked.

"What do you think a Gulag is exactly, sir?" The man was clearly growing tired of the interruptions. "The latest data we have suggests that there is a nuclear reactor on the island. I suggest you ask yourself what reasons the Russians could have for building something so expensive in such an isolated location."

"More ducks and elephants?"

"That's as may be, but the information we received

from Carlisle has put a rather more important spin on things. Hence this briefing. Our government has made an offer of assistance in rescuing the submarine and its crew, but the Russians have denied the existence of a submarine in the area let alone that there is one caught in the ice."

"Are you surprised by that? The Russians would rather see their men die than accept the help of anyone else. They won't dare show any weakness to the world. And the last thing they want is their tech falling into what they see as enemy hands."

"I'm not surprised at all, Commander. However, would it surprise you to learn our latest intelligence reports that a Spetsnaz team is being sent to the location of the *Echo II* sub? Their orders are to retrieve Pandora's Egg. Their mission brief is not to free the submarine; not even to rescue the crew. Their sole objective is to retrieve the Egg."

"Are you sure?"

"Carlisle was. That's good enough for us."

"And you think Pandora's Egg is some kind of weapon?"

"Crack the shell and unleash all of the evils of the world," Leopov said. That made them look her way again. "An *Echo II* submarine is equipped with Vulcan missiles. Wrangel Island puts it close enough to US soil to launch an attack. Now imagine something worse," she said, voicing the suspicion they were all thinking.

The man still standing at the front turned toward Leopov. Her heart leapt, pounding a little too fast in her chest, before she realized he was actually looking at the man beside her.

"Commander Maxwell. What's the status of your team?"

"They are already on route to Juneau, Alaska, and should be there in the next couple of hours."

"Excellent. Then their task is simple. They need to

locate the submarine and secure Pandora's Egg. There's a plane waiting to take you there. A helicopter will be on standby to take you to the ship. Your men will be on board."

The commander nodded. "Then what are we waiting for?"

"There's just one thing. I'd like you to take the Lieutenant with you."

"And why the hell would you want that? She's a number cruncher. No offense, my dear." He turned to Leopov and fixed her with an apologetic smile. "But I don't want to be responsible for getting you killed. And I really don't want you to be responsible for getting any of my men killed."

"She has local knowledge, no one knows the area better, and she speaks Russian with a perfect accent. Utilize all of the assets at your disposal, Commander."

"Whatever you say," the man beside her said.

He didn't take well to receiving orders from civilians.

THREE

Fog hung over the sea and ice like a white blanket, drifting on unseen breezes that offered the briefest glimpses of the nothingness that lay beneath and beyond.

Dane Maddock wasn't sure that he liked the look of it. They were still some distance from the island and already the ice floes were getting denser, the sheer weight of ice around them claustrophobic. The waters encircling Wrangel Island were Russian territory. They were already deep inside their jurisdiction. If word leaked of their presence here it would be considered a military incursion—an act of hostility. Given the gradual thaw in frosty relations between the two superpowers, that would be a disaster of epic proportions. He really didn't want to be the guy who broke Glasnost or Perestroika, whichever one it was that meant we were all getting along just fine now thank you very much.

He had been briefed on the fly about the intricacies of the situation: the island and the surrounding sea for twelve nautical miles were protected under international law and the Russians were quite happy using that as a reason for keeping ships at a distance. The gambit, not really the most convincing one Maddock had heard, basically came down to luck. The entire plan hinged on speed and the hope that the Red Army weren't paying too much attention to the seas because of other more pressing problems.

In and out, that was the plan. In and out.

Looking at the infinite ice, it was no surprise that a ship, even a nuclear submarine, could get itself locked in this frozen waste. It was bleak. The cold ate at his face, riming his stubble. The ice was thick, too. Cracks in the great plates showed that. Thick enough, surely, that even an ice breaker could get itself caught in the shifting sheets of ice. That would leave them at the mercy of the Russians. He didn't want to think about what that would mean for the team. Seeing out the rest of his life in a gulag didn't seem like a great career move. But, if the top brass were right and the island was being used for something the Russians didn't want the rest of the world to know about, it was a guarantee that's where the boys would end up.

"At least she's traveling light," Willis Sanders observed. The tall, broad-shouldered African-American wasn't looking out to sea.

"Not sure if I want to know whether you're talking about the ship or the Lieutenant," Maddock said, seeing Leopov leaning against the guard rail on the other side of the deck. There was something about a woman in uniform. She had, as Bones had so aptly phrased it, a body like a country road; loads of curves a guy would like to stop off and have a picnic on. Fitting in the Lieutenant's case. She was, however, obviously out of her depth and not happy to be bobbing about on the waves, crashing into the ice with suicidal abandon. Her eyes, so sparkling when they'd first met, now brimmed with dark concern, and her engaging smile was nowhere to be seen. It was understandable; to ignore, or even relish an environment like this took a special kind of madness like the one that afflicted the sailors she had hitched a ride with.

The helicopter had managed to reach the ship before the fog swallowed it completely. He wasn't sure why the woman was being forced upon them, but as long as she didn't get in the way of the mission, fine. She was obviously considered an asset by mission control. He was hardly going to call them idiots to their faces—not even over the safety of the ship-to-shore radio.

Their commander, Hartford "Maxie" Maxwell had only stayed on board for a couple of minutes, preferring to give his briefing face-to-face. That was his style. Look into the men's eyes. Don't ask them to do something you're not prepared to do yourself. He was a good man like that. That kind of leadership inspired faith. But until he'd actually laid down the mission brief, less than eighteen hours ago, they hadn't been remotely sure what was expected of them here, which was far from ideal.

Now that he *did* know, he liked it even less.

He didn't find the prospect of diving into these icy waters remotely appealing.

"The woman, of course. Come on, Maddock. It ain't like I'm a complicated man." Willis grinned broadly. "I ain't seen much gear shipped on board for her, so I figure she ain't equipped for combat even if she is front-loaded."

"Maxie says she's here for her language skills." Maddock shrugged. "She speaks Russian with native fluency."

Willis tilted his head and frowned. "Might be an asset if we stop around long enough to talk to anyone, I guess."

Maddock nodded. "I got the feeling there was some resistance to her coming along."

"Let me guess, it was her name right? Ignorance raises its ugly head again. If you've got the wrong kind of name, or the wrong accent you must be trouble."

"Or the wrong color skin?" Maddock raised an eyebrow.

"You know that's right. I keep telling you, Maddock. It pays to listen to me. I am wise beyond my years." Willis grinned, displaying straight, white teeth.

The ship jolted as it struck heavy ice, rising up before crashing back down in a huge sea-sickening lurch as both moved slowly through the water. The ship was designed for ramming a passage through sheets of polar ice. That didn't stop Maddock from feeling unnerved at the way the sound rang through the metal of the hull, growing louder instead of quieter as the hollow hull amplified it through some weird trick of acoustics. It sounded as if the metal was being torn apart down there. That made it hard not to imagine the ocean spilling in to fill the void and pulling the ship relentlessly under.

A nervous silence engulfed the deck as they waited for the next impact.

Maddock hadn't even noticed he was holding his breath until he let out a long slow sigh. They were still afloat. It was as if the ship held its breath too. It continue to drift and push against the ice, but now it did so in near silence. They'd cut the engines. The ship drifted only under its own momentum.

"Yo, Maddock. The captain says this is as close as he can get us," a voice called through the fog from somewhere further back on the deck.

"Bones?"

"You expecting someone else?" The hulking figure of Uriah "Bones" Bonebrake emerged from the mist. The Cherokee bore the deeply ingrained frown of a man who didn't enjoy the cold. Maddock could not blame him. Shame Russian submarines never ran aground in the Florida Keys or just off the coast of Hawaii.

"Where the hell are we?" Bones scowled at the horizon.

"Still a mile from the island itself, but the ice is packed so tightly that we're not going to be able to get much closer. By the time the ship comes to a halt we'll have pushed into solid ice."

"And?" Willis asked.

"End of the road. We walk from there." Maddock grimaced.

"Walk? Are you freaking kidding me?" Bones grumbled.

"I guess you could run if you really wanted to, but I'm thinking it'll be kind of slippery down there."

They had been prepared for this moment, of course. Their heavy polar clothing insulated them from the worst of the staggering cold, but the wind chill was the worst of it by far, easily ten degrees below anything remotely tolerable. Maddock was glad of the three day beard he'd managed to grow on the ship. It at least some kept some of the chill from his face, though it felt as if his lips shrank and tightened with every breath he took.

Even though the ships engines no longer turned, the momentum kept them gliding relentlessly forward for longer than he'd anticipated. The resistance of the ice floe slowed them, but it was gradual, and as their weight pushed them through fissures in the ice, it took an age to finally halt.

Rope ladders were thrown over the side. They scaled down them slowly. The rope was kinder on their grip than the iron ladder that ran part way down the hull. They wore thick fleece lined mittens with inner cotton linings, but the cold of the metal could have penetrated even that and frozen their gloves in place long before they reached the ice, and each rung on the ladder already thick with treacherous ice.

"This is it then?" Maddock asked when they finally stood on the ice. Bones and Willis seemed even larger in their protective clothing with thick soled boots and fur-lined hooded coats, like giant polar bears rearing up on the ice, and in the case of the two big men, every bit as intimidating. The captain had warned them about the danger of real polar bears, but looking at this pair, there was no way they'd want to go toe-to-toe for territory no matter how threatened they felt. He grinned, the smile lost in the rime around his chin. Beside Maddock, Pete Chapman, nicknamed "Professor" both for his intelligence and his broad knowledge of mostly useless trivia, shivered inside his own cold weather gear, slapping his hands against his arms as if it'd get his blood pumping.

"You all right, Professor?" Maddock asked.

Professor nodded, the gesture almost lost in his heavy hood. "Let's get this show on the road, shall we?"

"I'm ready when you are." Lieutenant Leopov assured them. "No need for special treatment, gentlemen." The Arctic clothing she'd been provided with smothered her slender frame.

"We really don't need you with us, Lieutenant," Maddock said. "We've got this one covered if you want to sit it out?"

"I've got my orders, just like you, and they say that I have to go with you wherever you go."

Maddock nodded. He looked into her eyes for a moment, her pale blue stare unblinking as she held his gaze. She was one determined woman.

"Say, Lieutenant, mind if I ask if you're here to spy on us?" Bones asked.

"Spy?"

"Yeah, you know, check up on us to make sure that we do things by the book. I mean, I figure you're not here to give lap dances or anything."

"There's a book?" She ignored the latter comment, obviously trying to pitch in with some levity in what could easily become uncomfortable, given the fact they'd be spending a lot of time together on the ice.

"So what are you doing here?" Bones pressed.

She took a second to answer that brutally direct question. She went for honesty in her reply. "I'm not sure why I'm here, solider, other than the fact that my being able to speak Russian might prove useful."

"Looking Russian can't hurt, either," Bones said.

"Must be in the genes," she said, the humor now absent from in her voice. "You know, given that my parents were Russian. I take it that's not going to be a problem?"

Maddock scanned their faces, trying to read their minds: they were about to head out into one of the most hostile climates in the world and the one thing they all needed to be able to do was trust their teammates. So much rested on what Bones said next.

"Not with me. You know which side you're on. That's all that matters." Bones gave her a wink.

"I do indeed. My father died getting my mother and me out of Russia. I know where my allegiance lies."

Bones nodded. And that was that. No dissent. She was more than capable of speaking up for herself. That was all the boys needed to know. Still, there was something about her that Maddock wasn't completely happy about, but he couldn't put his finger on it. It would have to wait. It would help to know why she was really there, because it couldn't be purely a language thing, no matter what Maxie had said. But if Maxie trusted her, it was enough for him.

A thoughtful look passed across Bones' face.

"What is it?" Maddock asked.

"I was just thinking. Leopov's got the Russian looks, you look Aryan with your blond hair and blue eyes, Willis and I have our obvious ethnic charms, but Professor," he turned to face Professor, "doesn't look like anything at all. What the hell are you, anyway?"

Indeed, there was nothing remarkable about Professor's lean build or light brown hair to make him stand out in a crowd.

"Scotch-Irish with a little French and a bit of..." Professor began.

"Nevermind." Bones raised a gloved hand. "I'm already bored."

"Let's roll," Maddock said. "But let's be clear about this, no making the natives restless if we can help it. The last thing we want is to have word of our arrival reaching the Russians before we've done our job. Our primary objective is getting the hell out of here in one piece." Maddock didn't need to say any more than that. They all knew what was expected of them—even the two new additions to the party. He motioned for them to lead the way. Nate Shaw and Seb Lewis had run missions like this even if they'd never run into Russian territory. They might not have the combat experience, but they were hostile environment experts. That made them worth their weight in gold here. He was glad to have them with him.

He gave one last glance at the ship. The risk was that the fog would make it difficult to find their way back. He took a bead on the coordinates. Looking up, he saw the Captain standing at the rail watching them head out on to the ice.

"Keep close together," he shouted, keen to make sure that he kept them all in sight. It was going to be hard enough to make their way across this surface without having to worry about losing anyone in the fog.

"This fog's thickening." Tension stretched Shaw's words. "It'd be smart to rope ourselves together, especially as the ice pack is shifting underfoot. We don't want anyone getting caught between the sheets. It's a lot less fun that it sounds."

"Is there a chance of that?" Bones asked.

Professor spoke up. "The ice isn't tightly packed, and it's constantly shifting, so yes, it could move under our feet at any time."

"Thanks for that." Bones looked down at the ground with an uneasy grin on his face. "I feel nice and calm now. How come you know so much about ice? I didn't think you'd been north of the Hudson?"

"He hasn't," Willis said. "But you know the Prof. If there's a book somewhere, he's read it."

Ragged laughter rippled through those assembled. The men knew each other well. It broke the tension, which was the whole point. They formed a link with the ropes to allow them to walk in single file. Everyone except the first and last man connected to two others who were no more than six feet away. They made their way forward slowly, stumbling from time to time. It took more than thirty minutes to cover less than a mile of shifting ice, and with every step it threatened to shift and pitch them into the icy water.

The first part of their journey ended when the feel of sold rock replaced the ice under their boots. Snow and ice still covered the landscape, but had the comforting feel of solidity.

Without the team even realizing it, the fog had thinned as they marched. They could see considerably farther than they'd been able to when they'd disembarked the ship, even with corkscrews of breath misting in front of their faces. Not that there was a lot to see beyond the whiteness of ice and snow. Only the occasional jagged edge of darker rock spearing up through the white surface broke the monotony.

"Where now?" Bones asked.

The fact that he felt the need to ask reminded Maddock how far they were from their comfort zone. In other situations he'd have simply looked for approval after making the suggestion himself. More often than not, he was the one Maddock looked to for his opinion. But this wasn't his territory. They might as well have been walking on the moon.

"West." Maddock grabbed the compass that hung from his belt, double checking that he had his bearings. He saw nothing to even suggest that man had stepped foot on this particular part of the island.

Nate Shaw led the way across the rough terrain, still cautious, planting each footstep with care. One misstep could be fatal. Maddock walked close behind him, keeping an eye on where he trod, making sure to follow in his footsteps. It was all about keeping the weight distribution on a solid foundation. If it held for one, it would hold for another. Even so, his feet slipped from time to time as he put his foot down on exposed rock. Amazingly, lichen grew on some of the stone, clinging on for dear life where there were so few signs of actual life to be seen.

Behind him, Leopov walked only a few feet away.

He felt her hand on his back twice as she steadied her balance. He didn't mind. That was what he was there for.

He turned a couple of times to see her walking with even more concentration than he was. At least she wasn't being careless.

Suddenly, Leopov gave out the slightest sound, a sharp sucking in of air.

Maddock turned to see her reaching out, one of her feet sinking down to the ankle where the surface wasn't as solid as she'd clearly thought.

He reached out one had to grab her flailing arm and kept her upright.

"Thanks." She pulled her boot from the hole that filled with water.

It was a stark reminder that although they were now on the island, rather than on the surface of the sea, and the ground was now solid enough to support their weight, they could easily be traversing a hidden river or any other kind of declivity that existed beneath the ice. One slip could have them pulled under.

He still held onto her hand as she took her next step.

Bones gave him a wry smile, making it obvious he thought Maddock's hand had lingered perhaps a moment too long.

"So how long have you been in the States?" he asked now that the ice had been broken in more ways than one.

"Almost all of my life," she said.

He listened as she offered some of her life story; how her father had been shot getting them out of the country, how she'd been made more welcome than she could have hoped. He wondered if that last bit were true given his team's reaction.

"And you ended up in Naval Intelligence?"

"It's a way of paying back." She offered no hint whether she meant paying back a debt of gratitude to the country that had given her and her mother a new life, or if she meant that she was paying Russia for killing her father. It didn't matter either way.

"How much further?" Professor called, his voice strangely eerie in the fog, as if it came from a hundred yards away despite the fact he followed less than five feet behind.

"Who knows?" Maddock said. "We need to set up camp so we can liaise with the ship to use each other as trig points to get the exact location of the submarine. They've been broadcasting a beacon, no doubt for the benefit of the Spetsnaz team. Be interesting to know if the crew realize they're still dead, whether the Spetsnaz guys reach them in time or not."

"*Shhhh*," came the hiss from Shaw, who still held the lead. He stood perfectly still, one arm held out from his side.

All Maddock heard was silence; not even the sound of breathing broke the stillness. He took a couple of steps forward so that he stood beside Shaw at the point. He could just make out a shape in the fog.

"We could have walked straight into that," Shaw whispered.

Although visibility had improved as they had walked, Maddock was surprised that they had drawn so close to buildings without being able to see them. He waited for a moment as the rest of the team huddled closer behind him; he could feel their presence and see warm breath drift over his shoulder.

"Wait here." He untied the rope that connected him to the group and took another cautious step forward, and another, trying not to make a sound as he approached. Ice still crunched underfoot with every step he took. Even a single sound could be enough to alert someone to the arrival of their uninvited guests. He slipped off his mitten and pulled out his Walther. Even through the thick gloves he wore as a lining to the mittens he could feel the bone-numbing coldness of the metal on his skin. Behind him, Bones brought his Glock to the ready.

"No shooting unless we have to," he said over his shoulder, then walked slowly away from them. Under normal circumstances he wouldn't have needed to give the order, but he didn't know Nate Shaw or Seb Lewis. He had no idea how they would react under pressure. And for that matter, he had no idea if Leopov was even carrying.

With each step the buildings became clearer, materializing in the fog. What at first had appeared as a huddle of low houses turned out to be a cluster of ramshackle structures that were seemingly held together by the elements that wouldn't let them fall apart. A few leaned against one another for support as if they would collapse if forced to support their own weight. There were no obvious signs of life. Stovepipe chimneys emerged from each roof, but not one of them billowed smoke to add to the fog. He felt his body relax as he realized that they hadn't stumbled onto a manned outpost. Whatever these building were, there hadn't been anyone home for a long time.

He turned and beckoned the others to join him but as he shifted his weight Maddock felt the ground give a little beneath his feet. The deep, resonant sound of a *crack* that reverberated all around him filled the silence between heartbeats. He didn't know whether to step back, or forward. Risked forward, but his foot slipped and a second sheering snap rang out. Too late he realized that he was standing on ice again, with nothing solid beneath his feet. The ice shifted and tilted, as if trying to buck him. It made it almost impossible to maintain his balance, the weight of the pack on his back threatening to pull him over. He tried a third step to relieve the pressure on the ice, but that only made things worse.

"Maddock!" someone shouted, but in his fight to keep

control he had no idea who. Water washed over the surface of the ice as his weight pressed down on it. He only had a moment to get off the unstable platform. He tried to take a step, but the ice supporting his standing foot slid beneath him and sent him plunging into the water.

He desperately tried to spread his arms across the rest of the ice that still clung to land, letting go of his gun as he went down. It couldn't save him, but clinging to the Walther sure as hell could kill him. The pistol skidded away from him as he kicked wildly, trying to find any kind of purchase to stop himself from sliding all the way into the ice cold water.

The tug of the current wasn't going to let him go.

It snatched at him, dragging him relentlessly down. He bobbed up back to the surface, spitting water, gasping and shivering, fighting not to be hauled away beneath the ice. Maddock knew that if he gave into it there would be no hope of getting out once that sheet of ice closed over his head. Even a few seconds down there could be lethal. The cold stole through his clothes, sucking the heat from him.

He needed to get out of there and he needed to get out fast.

His hands scrabbled against the jagged edge of the broken ice.

He could feel himself getting heavier and heavier as the water soaked into every pore, weighing him down. The pull was relentless. The ice in his bones hardened, making it impossible to fight it. Ice cracked again and gave way beneath his arms.

The cold swallowed him up.

Maddock's world turned black as he slipped beneath the ice.

FOUR

The cold water burned at his eyes. He couldn't open them, but he knew he had to.

There was nothing to see; not even a faint glow of light that should have come from the surface. He couldn't see the fissure he'd fallen through. Had it closed back over his head? He struggled in futility against the overwhelming darkness.

Was this the end? Drowning was supposed to be pleasant. Better than a bullet, at least. He closed his eyes again.

No! He would not give in. Not yet, anyway. His lungs strained at his ribs, close to bursting as he struggled to hold that last breath the cold was so desperate to shock out of them. He knew that he could ease the pain by letting the air leak out of his mouth. But without oxygen he'd go down fast. Besides, he couldn't part his lips; the message wasn't reaching his extremities, that or his body knew better than to take any notice of the panic fighting for control of it.

His arms and legs flailed, battling uselessly against the current that would wash him out toward the deeper sea if he gave himself to it. He kicked against the undertow, giving every ounce of strength he had remaining to the fight. It bought him a few feet, then lost one as the water pushed him back.

He was drowning.

He knew it.

The light above him changed for a moment. Light? Or were those spots exploding across his mind's eye as oxygen deprivation killed him? Conflicting thoughts swarmed across his mind—don't go into the light, swim for the light. Embrace the afterlife, live damn it, live. He wanted to live, whichever choice that was. He wasn't ready to die, not like this. He surged upward, toward the light and reached out, his hand thrusting up through the ripples into the air. Someone grabbed at him, catching hold of his upper arm before he could sink back down beneath the surface again. He reached for the hand, praying that it was a hand, not some sort of Arctic seaweed.

He couldn't panic. Panic could drag his savior beneath the ice rather than lift him out.

Another pair of hands grabbed hold of his arm as the last of his strength ebbed away. He lost the last breath he'd been holding onto.

His body fell limp.

A moment later his head burst through the surface of the water and he found himself gasping for air, still very much alive. Voices demanded to know if he was all right, but it was all he could to do breathe as the air burned his lungs and he thought for the first time, seriously, that he was going to die because he couldn't stand the pain.

He coughed and spat out a lungful of the ocean as someone hauled him clear of the icy water and onto dry land. Bones wasn't letting go of him.

"Thanks," he managed between raking shudders. It was barely enough, but it he had nothing more to give at the moment.

The big man just nodded.

Maddock lay on his back, staring up at the sun where it pierced the pervasive shroud of mist. Some small part of his subconscious imagined it to be the light toward which dying people drifted as life fled their bodies.

"We need to get you out of these clothes," Professor said. He mumbled something about hypothermia being the biggest killer out here, but he could have been speaking through a woolen blanket. Maddock's head throbbed and ached with the cold as he felt the moisture that had caught in his stubble start to freeze, seeming to crush his skull with the sudden intensity of it.

"Easy Professor," said Bones. "Let's try and find somewhere to get him warm before we start stripping him down to his tightie whities. This isn't the place for standing around naked." Besides, imagine the shrinkage this cold weather has caused.

Maddock almost managed a grin, but his lips were frozen in place.

Professor gave Maddock a long look, then turned to Bones. "Bring him down to the buildings. I'll go ahead and find the best place to get a fire going."

Maddock felt Bones grab hold of him around his waist and haul him to his feet. Bones draped one of Maddock's limp arms around his shoulder and got him moving. Maddock went with it. Professor was right. It would have been easier for the big man to throw him over his shoulder fireman-style, but Bones was letting Maddock keep some of his dignity. Should his legs buckle, that would change.

He was starting to feel that he should be able to cover the short distance under his own steam, but the strength disappeared from his legs within a dozen steps. It was all he could do to stop his teeth chattering. And even that was a struggle he couldn't win. He could scarcely keep a thought in his head for more than a moment. He needed to get some heat back under his skin and that wasn't going to happen in these soaking clothes.

The buildings lay less than four hundred yards across the ice. Those four hundred yards were some of the most arduous he'd ever walked. Each step sent a shiver of pain through muscles that were shrinking in the cold, pulling themselves tighter and tighter.

"Let me carry you," Bones said. They'd barely gone fifty feet. Maddock shook his head. He needed to put one foot in front of another to keep going. Get the blood moving again. If he couldn't even do that much he would be of no use to anyone.

Some of the team found it hard to hang back with them, face into the wind, with shelter so close.

"If you want to make yourself useful go see what you can do to help Professor get that damn fire going," Bones growled. "Scavenge whatever fuel you can, even if that means pulling one of the buildings apart with your bare hands, get that fire burning."

Shaw and Lewis hurried ahead, grateful for the chance to get out of the wind. Leopov hesitated for an instant before following along behind them. Only Willis hung back.

When they were out of earshot Bones paused and readjusted his grip. "You hanging in there, bro?"

"Just about," Maddock replied, or thought he did. He couldn't be sure his lips had even moved enough to enunciate the words beyond a mumble.

That was good enough for Bones.

"Well now that there's just you and me out here, how about you give up some of that stubborn pride of yours and you let me carry you the rest of the way? I really don't want to freeze my ass off out here any longer than I have to."

Maddock shook his head.

"At least let me help." Without waiting for a reply, Willis ducked beneath Maddock's free arm and he and Bones began to haul their frigid comrade forward.

Maddock moved his feet, but there was little need. The tips of his boots scarcely skimmed the surface of the frozen ground as the two big men swept him forward. At just under six feet tall, Maddock stood a few inches shorter than Willis and half a foot shorter than Bones, but right now he felt like a child being carried along. At least he remained upright and could maintain the illusion of carrying a bit of his own weight, though for whose benefit he couldn't say.

Maddock felt the warm lure of unconsciousness tugging at him, trying to draw him into the realm of sleep. But that was no place he wanted to be, even if it would be warmer there, and he'd be free of the pain in his legs. It was important he stay clear. Alert. Awake. He counted each jolting footstep that Bones and Willis took, each one taking them closer to the buildings; each one meaning that he drew closer to the warm and dry. The effort must have been causing every muscle in the men's bodies to strain, but it didn't show. They were rock solid men, physically and mentally. Even Bones, who was as reckless and foolish as they came when off-duty, but over time, Maddock had gained a grudging respect for the big Cherokee's skills in the field.

When they were a few strides from the door leading into the building Professor had picked, Bones and Willis lowered him to the ground, still supporting his weight, and helped him to make the last few steps on his own. He was grateful for the charade.

A fire had already begun to take hold in the hearth. The sharp tang of wood smoke and the welcome wave of warm, dry air greeted him. Wood crackled and fizzed as flames licked into the air. He had no idea where they'd found the wood. He didn't care. All he cared about was getting warm, even if the air felt no different than it had done beyond the threshold. It would, soon. And just knowing that was enough to get him as far as the chair beside the fireplace. He slumped into it as Bones eased his support away.

Concerned faces gathered round.

He tried to retain his tenuous grip on consciousness, but eventually there was nothing he could do but surrender.

He felt rough hands on him as his wet clothes were pulled away. He didn't resist. His limbs were numb, muscles useless, but there was no longer anything he could do about it. He was in the care of others.

He dreamed of ice closing in above him.

FIVE

Maddock awoke lying on the floor. He felt the warmth of the fire on his skin. As his senses grew more alert, the sound of muffled voices slowly became clearer.

He opened his eyes to see the wood lying in the hearth had blackened and charred and now glowed with a deep warm red at its core. It gave off enough heat to sting his face. He tried to move. The voices stopped suddenly. He knew that meant he was the center of attention. Every joint ached as he tried to sit up, every muscle filled with pain. It felt as if they hadn't moved in days.

"How are you feeling?"

He moved too quickly, his head pounding as he tried to sit up. He couldn't even be sure who had spoken, so addled were his senses.

"I'm fine," he lied trying to hold back the darkness that swam at the edge of his vision. He pulled himself up into the chair again, wondering how he'd ended up on the floor, and took the opportunity to look around properly. Bones and Professor were sitting at small table, but neither of them made the slightest move toward him. Plates and mugs lay scattered across the table, bearing food debris. At first he thought the others had fed themselves while he had been out of it but then he realized that the plates had been there for some time. The edges of the scraps of bread were white with frost burn. This was the previous residents' last supper, or the remnants of it at least. The cabin's previous occupants had apparently walked out into the endless winter and abandoned the place. Had they expected to return? Or had they just left in a hurry? Without the familiar bacteria and mold growths it was impossible to tell how long the place had been empty. Months? Years?

"How long was I out it?" he croaked.

Bones glanced at his watch. "Half an hour, maybe a little more."

It could have been worse, but half an hour was a long time when they were in a race against time, or at least a race against the Russians. They couldn't afford to be sitting around and doing nothing, waiting for him to thaw out.

"Where's everyone else?" He hadn't realized they were down in numbers until then. The room wasn't big enough to hide anyone. He was slowly coming back to himself.

"I sent them out to scout the area and make sure that there's no one hiding out in these buildings. They should be back before long. I didn't think you'd want them all to see you naked. You're not the most impressive physical specimen."

Maddock hadn't even realized he wasn't wearing the same clothes he'd been in when he went under the ice. He saw them now, a wet pile on the floor beside the fire.

"Your mom thinks I look pretty good," he rasped.

"He's already feeling better," Bones said.

"Here." Professor handed him a plastic beaker. "Drink up. It's still hot."

Even the steam from the coffee, strong and black, felt good as he raised it toward his lips. The first sip burned, but he wasn't about to let that stop him. He savored the heat as it trickled down inside him, coming alive again.

"What about Lieutenant Leopov?"

"First one out of the door," Bones laughed "I think she's got something to prove, or at least thinks she has."

"Do you think that was a good idea?" Maddock took another sip of the hot, bitter liquid.

"Why?"

"I don't know, but it's probably best to keep her close. Maybe she *can* speak Russian maybe that's exactly why she's here, but I've got this sneaking suspicion there's more to it than that."

"It doesn't make her one of the bad guys though," Professor said.

"Ah, Professor, don't let legs that go straight on 'til morning distract you," Bones said, a sly smile spreading across his face.

"It's not that, it's just..."

"Don't rise to it. He's yanking your chain." Maddock stretched, easing the kinks out of his back, then took another slug of coffee. The Cheshire Cat smile on Bones' face seemed to stretch even wider. It was a miracle he didn't disappear into a puff of smoke, leaving nothing but that toothy grin behind. Professor's expression didn't change.

"So what do we do now?" Bones asked.

"We didn't want to get too far ahead of ourselves until you were back in the land of the living," Professor said.

"We wait until the others get back. Unless they have anything to report, we establish this as our base, then we send out a scouting party to look further afield. We can't afford to be hanging around."

"Roger that." Bones gave him a level look. In his eyes, Maddock read an unspoken question.

"I'm fine. Really." Privately, Maddock hoped that was the truth.

SIX

They moved from building to building, securing one point before moving onto the next.

Leopov was already convinced that there was no one else in this godforsaken ninth circle of hell, but the men were methodical, following a routine that had been drilled into them. This was not part of her world, not something she had been exposed to before, at least not in any kind of meaningful way where there was the risk that one mistake could leave you, back turned to a real live gunman. She had been through basic training, but nothing that could have prepared her for this. She had been recruited into intelligence before any risk of being thrown into a combat zone ever became a reality. To the other men around her this was, or at least had been, a way of life.

She was in their hands.

She had no intention of doing anything other than what they told her to do, and doing that to the letter.

The door of the next shack along hung open.

Snow and ice had drifted inside giving the whole floor a covering of white that crunched underfoot as she entered. She saw no sign of life inside, no sign of anyone having been there for weeks, months, perhaps even longer. A single stool lay upturned beside the sink.

"Stay there," Willis said.

She waited for the few moments it took him and Shaw to check the rest of the building while Lewis waited outside with her. There was very little to check. She would have preferred to have stayed inside the room where the fire was starting to win the fight to stay alive, but she knew that would be failing in her mission. She had been tasked to discover whatever she could about the Russian operations on the island provided she could do it without putting herself in danger. And she wanted Maddock's team to trust her. Trust wasn't automatic. You earned it. Hence coming out here. The rest of the team were more than capable of carrying out the mission, but she was acting as the eyes and ears of those higher up the chain of command. She didn't like having secrets from the men to whom she had entrusted her life, but her orders had been clear. It was need-to-know and they didn't need to know.

"Clear," Willis said as he re-emerged into the main room. "Let's move on."

Leopov took one last look around, but there was nothing to learn there; nothing to tell her who might have been staying in this place, why they had been there or why they'd left. Maybe it had been used as an outpost for the Russians. It could just as easily have been the home for a few families eking out an existence from whatever they could fish up from beneath the ice. Whichever it was, it didn't look as if it had been much of a life.

The next three building were the same. In one they found a photograph of a small girl and a pair of handprints in green paint on a piece of paper taped to the wall. It was the first thing she'd seen that was even remotely personal. They found odds and ends of possessions in the other huts, but all had been practical. This showed that there had been someone real here; ordinary people living mundane lives. The revelation only added to the disquiet she felt knowing that they had left behind things that they probably thought precious.

If there had been locks on any of the shacks, none of them had been secured. Each time they were able to push the doors open once they'd overcome the resistance of frozen and rusted hinges. Only one building remained secure; a square structure constructed from concrete blocks. Snow had drifted up against one side of it, partly obscuring the single door. Willis placed a gloved hand on the handle and tried to turn it. It moved a little, but the door wasn't budging an inch.

"Locked?" Leopov asked. As the words left her lips she half expected a sarcastic reply, but instead he just nodded and stepped back.

"You want me to go and find something to open it?" Shaw asked.

"Naw, man," Willis said. "I've got it covered."

He pointed his gun at the lock.

Leopov instinctively took a couple of steps back.

She was not particularly fond of guns, no matter how familiar she might have been with them. It was something she had to deal with; something she couldn't avoid coming into contact with, given her stock in trade, but it didn't mean that she had to like them. Respect them, yes. Be familiar with handling them, absolutely, but like them? No. By the third shot the wood around the lock on the door was splintered and the handle hung off to the side.

"Back in Detroit we call this an urban skeleton key," Willis smiled. "It opens just about anything one way or another."

He pushed the door wide open.

The building had been locked, but that didn't mean abandoned or occupied. Simply locked. No risks. They were doing this by the book, sweeping the place. One thing was sure though, if anyone waited inside, they now knew they had visitors.

Leopov felt her heart beating in her chest as if it was banging on her ribs in an attempt to force a way out.

She waited outside for a moment as the men went in.

Counting it out until she heard someone calling to her.

"Lieutenant," the voice said first, then more urgently. "Hey, Leopov!"

It was the first time that anyone had used her name. It wasn't her first name, but these guys didn't use first names. It was a landmark moment, but she wasn't going to relish it. She was still an outsider, even if they knew her name.

But she had a chance to become part of the team, at least for the duration of this mission.

"Coming." She trusted them to have given the place a thorough sweep and made sure it was clean.

As she entered the first room she heard a voice she did not recognize.

It spoke in Russian.

SEVEN

The sound of gunfire silenced Maddock, Bones and Professor for a moment, but in the long sliding echo that followed they were on their feet and shrugging themselves into their coats and stepping into boots. Maddock's coat still felt heavy from water, but it was almost dry on the inside; it was the only item of clothing that he hadn't brought a spare of. He snatched up his gun without slipping on his holster, and stepped outside. There was no way of knowing what lay out there, but they wouldn't be shooting unless there was a damned good reason for it, like a bunch of Spetsnaz thugs trying to fill their bodies with lead.

"You stay here," he whispered to Professor, "and hold down the fort. Bones and I will check it out." Professor grimaced but nodded his acquiescence.

Maddock took a few steps, the chill wind battering his weakened body. He paused and cocked an ear. Sound travelled in a strange way in this place, making it difficult to know which way they should go.

He held Bones back with one straight arm as they moved forward.

If they could identify the problem without alerting anyone else to their presence, that would be a win. If the threat was Spetsnaz, better if they didn't know there were more men and more guns to deal with than they'd faced so far. Better to be smart than lucky. Always.

Maddock pressed himself tight against the wall of the shack, his Walther at the ready as he reached the corner of the building. He held a finger to his lips, then motioned for Bones to cover the next point. The air echoed with the sound of footsteps moving quickly. They were getting closer by the moment.

Maddock signaled for Bones to hold back.

They had a good position. They were ready for whoever it was. Maddock tensed as a figure barreled around the corner. He recognized the man immediately.

"Nate!" Maddock hissed as Shaw thundered toward them.

"We've got something." The point man sucked on the cold air as he struggled to catch his breath. "This way."

Maddock called for Professor to join him and Bones. They followed close behind Shaw, Maddock keeping pace despite the ache in his joints. It was getting easier with each stride. It felt good to be moving. He saw the door to the concrete building hanging open and stopped.

"It's all clear," Shaw said.

Maddock frowned. "We heard shooting."

"Willis used a little extra force to open the door. We'd checked all the other buildings and they were clear. This was the only one that was locked. We guessed it had been secured for a reason."

"And?"

"You'd better see for yourself." Shaw stepped back and invited Maddock to walk inside.

The interior lay in gloom, contours of shadow picking out the shapes of furniture. Someone was speaking Russian but he couldn't see anyone.

It took him a second to realize the voice emanated from a radio.

He saw Leopov sitting beside the base unit, listening intently to the words crackling out of the speaker.

"What's he saying?"

"It's a distress call." Her eyes narrowed in concentration as she concentrated on the words. "It's not live though. It's being broadcast on a loop."

"Can we get a fix on it?" Maddock asked.

"I'll get in touch with the ship," Professor said. "If they can pick up the signal we might be able trace it back to a location, but I wouldn't hold your breath. Best hope, we might be able to get hold of someone with access to a satellite. Maybe Big Brother back home can get a fix on it."

"Assuming it's the sub," Maddock said. "We know the Russians will be monitoring the frequency. We just contact the ship, you know the drill. If we try to make contact with home base there's more chance the Russians will hear. Do what you can. If you can't, such is life. There's more than one way."

"I'm on it," Professor headed back to the shack they'd set up their base camp in. The Russians would already know exactly where the submarine was and would be heading straight for it, no need for stealth or subterfuge. They weren't the ones risking an international incident.

"It's not a standard SOS," Leopov said. "There's more to it than that."

"Go on."

"They're not just trapped in the ice. They're dying."

"What?"

"They're dying," she said again. "There was some kind of accident. The members of the crew are all falling ill and dying. They need help."

"They're on a nuclear sub," Bones said. "Any kind of accident that has people dying is a game changer. Are you sure about this?"

Leopov nodded. "I'm sure. We should try to help them."

Maddock shook his head. "That's not the mission." He wasn't sure if he believed that himself. Yes, they had had their orders just as the Russians did. Men were dying out there. It was an *Echo II* class nuclear sub. It had an onboard reactor. What the hell kind of accident were they talking about?

What was he leading the team into?

EIGHT

"All right, what have we got, Professor?" Maddock asked when the man returned to the shack.

Professor had plugged a headset into the radio they had brought with them, and was listening intently to what he was being told over the wire. He scribbled a series of numbers on the edge of the map he'd spread out on the table, the remnants left behind by the previous occupants still in place beneath it. He nodded a couple of times, despite the fact that no one on the other end could see him. When he had finished writing, he pulled off the headset and looked up.

"We've got a rough location. It's pretty sketchy but they're trying to pinpoint it by moving the ship to another location. As long as the transmission keeps getting repeated they'll use it for triangulation. That should get us a little closer."

"Show me." Maddock instructed.

Professor worked with a quick efficiency. He marked their position on the map with a simple cross then added another for the approximate position of the ship. He checked the two rows of figures he'd penciled at the side of the map and drew in two lines, one from each of the two crosses until they intersected. "It's not as accurate as it might be, because we are still fairly close to the ship. But it's a ballpark. The captain's going to move her around to the east end of the island and get us another reading. That should help us pinpoint the sub."

"We don't have the luxury of time, Professor," Maddock said. "*Pretty sure* is going to have to be good enough. We just need to get moving in the right direction. If the ship can improve on the data all well and good, but we will at least be closer to the submarine by then. How far are we talking?"

"Twenty five klicks, but it's not only a matter of how far." Professor traced his finger along the line from their current position. "The signal is coming from the other side of the coastal plain and that means crossing the Tsentral'nye Mountain Range. That's going to be a bear of a hike. And not just because it's cold out there."

"I think we all know just how cold it is out there." Bones shuddered as he spoke. "I've dated church girls who weren't this frigid."

Professor scowled. "We've not come close to cold yet, Bones. We're talking as low as minus twenty six up there."

"Chilly," Bones agreed. "Couldn't we take the scenic route and go around the mountains then? Save us a few degrees of frostbite?"

"Man, that would, like, double the distance." Willis scowled and shook his head. "It's going to be tough enough to cover twenty five klicks in a single day as it is. Fifty? Ain't no way. We might as well just let the Russkies have the egg."

"Agreed. We can't afford to waste that much time, not if we want to get this thing done." Maddock said. "Every hour we lose increases the risk that they'll beat us to the punch."

"It's already starting to get dark out there." Bones turned back from the cabin's grime-dark window. "You're not seriously suggesting that we try and negotiate a freakin' iced-up mountain range at night? The cold's frozen your brain, chief."

"Realistically, we're going to be out there at night regardless, whether it's actual night or not, and not by choice," said Professor. "At this time of year this place only gets a few hours of daylight, max. By the time we reach the range, even if we set off at dawn, it'll be getting dark, and then we'd be kicking back with no shelter, freezing our asses off for the fun of it. Think of it this way, rather dark than foggy."

Maddock wasn't so sure, but it wasn't as if they had a whole heck of a lot of choice in the matter. The objective was clear—beat the Russians to Pandora's Egg. This was what they did. This was why command paid them the very small bucks. He nodded to Professor. "Then we have to get as far as we can tonight, be ready for when the sun comes up to get across those peaks. We've got bivouacs, and everything we need for a couple of nights in the open."

"Then we'd better get ready to ship out."

Maddock gave Leopov the briefest of glances. This wasn't the kind of adventure he wanted her tagging along on, if he was honest. He was thinking about her safety primarily. "It's going to be rough out there, Lieutenant."

"I'm coming with you," she said, "Don't even think about trying to talk me out of it. This isn't the 1950's. There's no weaker sex here."

"I guess she told you, Maddock." Bones chuckled and gave Leopov an approving look.

Maddock nodded. There was no point in arguing. He only hoped they weren't borrowing trouble in bringing Leopov along.

Time would tell.

NINE

The fog had lifted before they cleared the outskirts of the village. Maddock had considered leaving a man behind to maintain the fallback position and assure the team had an exfiltration route if worst came to worst without stretching their resources too thinly. The reality of the situation though, was that they needed to stick together. As a unit the chances of success increased. It wasn't some dumb hero quest; it was a mission that would demand all of their individual skill sets if they were going to beat the Russians. Besides, breaking up the team would mean trying to coordinate some kind of rendezvous out on the ice, likely with the Russians chasing at least one party, if they were going to get back to the ship. Not ideal.

The clear night sky spread out above them—jewels sparkling on a blanket of black. Moonlight reflected from the ice, setting the world in an ethereal glow. Boots crunched through the virgin surface. A sense of loneliness unlike anything he'd ever experienced pervaded this frozen landscape. It was so cold he barely felt it. He recognized the danger—a sign that his threshold had been broken. It wasn't about tolerance. It should *feel* cold. At minus twenty it should feel like hell well and truly had frozen over.

Professor led the way with his GPS device in hand, the map folded and tucked into his pocket of his goose down four-season jacket. There were twenty four satellites up there feeding back info to the Department of Defense HQ and triangulating their global position through the wonders of Star Wars level tech Maddock wasn't interested in as long as it worked. He was, however, well aware that Korean Airlines Flight 007 had been shot down by the Russians a few years back for mistakenly venturing into their sovereign air space, killing two hundred sixty nine civilians. What they would do confronted with a military incursion didn't bear thinking about. They couldn't risk being caught.

The first flew klicks passed relatively painlessly, save for the numbing cold and the burn of the pack straps on their shoulders. That changed when the mountains came into sight. The team lapsed into silence. Only the slow steady crunch of snow and ice underfoot sounded above the howling wind.

Maddock could see that Leopov was starting to tire. Her steps were labored and her expression grim, but she was stubborn. She matched their pace without complaint. Good for her. He dropped back to walk beside her. He didn't want the team stringing out. Bones would set the pace, he'd bring up the rear and make sure no one was left behind.

"You hanging in there?" he asked, holding out an arm for her to hang onto as the ice shifted beneath her feet. She didn't take it.

"I'm fine," she said, as she regained her footing.

"Okay, Lieutenant, I'm going to ask you something. It's just us here, so be straight with me."

"Shoot."

"Have you told me everything?" He had no problem about the team listening in, but figured it'd be easier for her to talk openly if it was just the two of them, and he knew full well this might be the only chance he got to talk to her alone before they crossed the mountains.

"I've told you, Maddock, I'm just here to observe and do what I can should the opportunity arise."

"Of course you are. No doubt you're also under orders not to tell me what your actual orders are, yes? Don't worry. You don't need to answer that. I understand orders. If you can't tell me, I get it, but I was told that you were with us because you could speak Russian."

"That's right." She met his gaze, her eyes daring him to

challenge her.

"Okay, so about that message. Have you told me everything?"

The expression on her face changed to something akin to relief. It was enough to convince Maddock that whatever she was hiding had nothing to do with the message. That was something, at least.

"I've told you everything, word for word, except..." She paused and glanced up at the night sky.

"Except?"

"All right, there was something weird about the intonation. My guess, they knew what it was that was making them ill."

"Right. Maybe not so surprising?"

"I don't know. Honestly. There was panic in his voice. I think he knew that whatever it is that they are suffering from was going to kill them all. It was fatalistic, you know? Like the cavalry couldn't save them no matter how fast it got there."

Maddock nodded. He tried to put himself in their place. How would he feel leading men in that situation? Trapped underwater, the air scrubbers failing and every likelihood that carbon dioxide poisoning would kill them before anything else. It would explain the panic and the fatalism.

"And it was definitely on a loop?"

She nodded. "You could even hear a click every time in started again."

He hadn't noticed. "Sounds like this is the kind of stuff you are used to listening into."

"It's more than just listening to the words," she said. "Even if you learn to speak a second language it doesn't mean that you can catch every inflection, language is nuanced, every sound carries additional meaning. You need to be able to speak it like a native. You have to live with it to understand it."

He nodded. "And you have?"

"My mother. She couldn't speak a word of English when she got to America. Neither could I. At home we spoke Russian even after I started school."

"Was it just you and your mother?"

It was good to get her talking. Put her at ease. Take her mind off the punishing journey ahead of them. It didn't hurt him either. Maddock listened as she told him about her father being killed while he was trying to get them out of the country. It seemed that America had welcomed them with open arms, but there was an undercurrent to it all, like she thought they'd have been better looked after if her father had made it out alive. He'd been a valuable asset.

"Did you have to leave anyone else behind?"

"Everyone. We left everyone behind." Was that bitterness or the wind stealing away the last sounds of the words? Every nuance and inflection was important. She'd said as much.

He wanted to push further, but he couldn't imagine her telling him more than she was willing to offer. It wasn't an interrogation. The question he couldn't shake was: was what she brought to the team worth the risk she was adding to the mission? The team could only move at the pace of the slowest member. She was it.

"You didn't have to hold back on my account," she said, reading his mind.

"Actually I do. That's exactly what I do need to do," Maddock replied. "I can't afford for you to fall behind. It's not too late to arrange for the ship to pick you up if you can't handle it. Don't let pride wind up getting someone killed, Lieutenant. We're a long way from home."

She didn't answer. Instead she strode out, planting one foot in front of another and driving on. Maddock had seen this kind of thing before; she was being driven on by a mixture of anger and determination. He'd just hit the right button. It might not last for long; right now there was no way she was going to be the last man through the gate. He could hear the effort in every step she took. He matched her pace for pace.

The others had bunched together and were looking back toward them. They'd gained a couple of hundred yards on them, closing the gap with each step. The mountains were closer. He had no idea if it was psychological, but it already felt much colder here as he trudged into the shadow of their slope.

"Take five," he said when they reached the others.

Leopov almost collapsed onto the packs the others had laid down while they'd been waiting. Someone poured her a beaker of coffee and handed it to her. It was going to be hard for her to get going again if they rested for too long. The others were already itching to get moving again before the weather worsened. They wanted to make the most of the shifting light, too. But standing still in the extreme cold meant the heat was getting away from them. Movement meant warmth. It was a very simple equation.

Bones and Willis began to pace, and soon wandered away.

"Not too far," Maddock barked.

"Yes, Dad." Bones called back.

Maddock shook his head and turned to Professor.

"How far have we covered?"

Professor fussed over the map. He checked it against the coordinates on his GPS.

"Just shy of seven klicks." He stole a glance at the girl. She was oblivious to the fact that they were thinking about her. It was those words, shy of, that betrayed his frustration. Maddock knew that Bones would keep it to himself, but no doubt felt the same. He had to make a decision before it became a problem.

Distance was hard to gauge in a landscape of unrelenting white. The ice glistened in the moonlight as if it reflected the stars, and closer to the horizon the higher ground looked like a vague darkness that merged with the sky.

"Not even halfway then," he said to himself. That was the reality of it. It had been hard going and they weren't even close to their goal. Professor said nothing. They both knew that they weren't moving anywhere near fast enough.

"Yo! Check this out!" Bones called.

The SEALs all whirled about in alarm, but Maddock could tell by the tone of Bones' voice that nothing was amiss.

"It's cool," he assured them. "Shaw and Lewis, you two stay with Leopov. Professor and I will see what's up."

They trudged the short distance to where Bones and Willis stood gazing at a snow and encrusted embankment.

"What is it?" Maddock asked.

"See for yourself." Bones pointed to an oddly-shaped crystal curving down out of a dark patch of exposed rock.

Curved crystal? That made no sense. Maddock moved in for a closer look and, with a start, realized what he was seeing.

"It's a wooly mammoth! A baby," he marveled.

"Seriously?" Professor reached out and brushed at what Maddock had taken to be the rock but was, in fact, the mammoth's head. "It's remarkably well-preserved. It must be thousands of years old, but it looks like it could have died here last week."

"Wrangel Island is supposed to be the last sanctuary for the mammoth," Bones said. "They were here as recently as two thousand B.C."

"How do you know that?" Maddock asked, surprised at the unexpected source of this fact.

"I'm into mysteries, legendary creatures, all that stuff. Some Native American tribes claim that the mammoth survived in North America until just before the white man arrived. I picked up the detail about Wrangel Island in my reading." He frowned at Maddock. "I wish you wouldn't look at me like that every time I mention that I read."

"You can't deny you've earned my skepticism," Maddock said.

"Whatever." Bones shook his head. "Anyway, I thought you'd want to see this. It's pretty cool, huh?"

They examined the exposed bit of the prehistoric creature for a few minutes longer before heading to rejoin the rest of their team.

Bones fell back beside Maddock, letting Willis and Professor take the lead. "How are you doing?"

"I'll survive. Don't worry about me." It felt like a lifetime ago since Maddock had taken his dip in the icy water. "You don't think I was holding her back do you?"

Bones held his hands up with his palms toward Maddock. "Hey, I didn't say a thing."

"Riiight." Maddock dragged the word out. He wished that he could put the same big smile on his face, but right then all he could think about was how they were going to get across the mountains. He hadn't even got to the part where he worried about beating the Russians to the stranded sub. "We should get moving again, though we probably shouldn't go much longer before we get some rest. Why don't we give you a ten minute head start so you can find a place to set up camp? You should have everything unpacked by the time we get to you."

Bones nodded and set about rounding up the others. He made sure that the packs were distributed evenly amongst them once more and led them out.

TEN

Maddock kept the others in sight.

Leopov had been on her feet the moment the main party had set off, but he'd made her rest a few extra minutes. They wouldn't be able to keep up with them, they both knew it, so better to conserve their strength than burn it.

"Don't worry. They'll have things set up for us when we get there. Think of it as one of the perks of the job."

Scorn marred her lovely face. "Right. That's one way of looking at it. Another is that you're making sure that I don't get under your feet."

He shrugged, smiled, though he doubted that she would be able to see the motion beneath the great fur-lined hood he wore. "Stick with me, kid. Orders are orders, right?"

She paused for a moment, then answered with a single nod. Her head moved more than the hood of the coat that swamped her.

So he was right. She'd been ordered to observe him, not just the operation.

He wasn't sure if that changed things. But, if he was going to be the object of her affection he'd just have to figure out a way to work with it.

Trailing behind while others carried the heaviest of the packs gave him to time to think, but short of tying her up he was not sure what he could do.

The others were in danger of moving out of sight. Maddock knew Bones would be well aware of their progress and doing his best to match it. If they became completely detached one of them would wait until they made visual contact. If Leopov was so determined to stay with them she either had to prove that she could do it, or determine once and for all she couldn't. He extended his stride and gradually increased the cadence of his walk. She tried to keep up, but the strain soon began to show.

"Fast, Lieutenant," he said. "Lives depend on it."

She made no reply. He could hear her labored breathing. She was stubborn, but tiring fast and each stride became increasingly harder than the one before.

Her legs buckled more than once. This time he didn't offer a hand to help her up. He maintained his pace, forcing her to keep on moving until she was almost breaking into a run just to try and match him.

"Is this how it's going to be then?" she asked, words coming out two or three at a time between freezing breaths. The mist punctuated each little parcel of words like commas in the air between them. "Get to the submarine before the Russians or die in the attempt?"

"That's exactly how it always has been," he said. "It's pretty much par for the course for us."

He was already three paces ahead of her. He wouldn't look back as long as he could still hear her labored breathing and the crunch of her footsteps. He knew she was with him. Maddock fought against the searing ache in his joints and the burning in his chest as the frigid air bit and clawed all the way down into his lungs, dragging down the warm inside of his throat to coat it with more and more frost with every breath. He knew somewhere in the back of his mind he was being just as unreasonable and stubborn as Leopov, but he wasn't about to ease up. They had an objective. This was easy going compared with what lay ahead. He needed to test himself. He needed to be sure he was up to it every bit as much as the girl.

When the first sight of a tent came into a view, the mottled gray and white nylon scarcely visible against the white of the ice and snow, he was the one who felt the first stirrings of relief. He used it to spur himself on, again increasing the cadence in his stride, pushing himself to a punishing rhythm.

He'd been lost in thought for too long, concentrating on the whiteness in front of him and the back of the man he could make out in the distance. He thought it was Bones, but it was impossible to tell and the landscape offered no visual indicators as to just how large—or small—the figure was. Following the man in front had meant that the sound of Leopov following him had been replaced by the sound of his own heart beat pounding in his ears, and the rasp of every ragged breath he took.

He tried to listen for her. Nothing.

He glanced back to see just how far she was behind him.

Almost a hundred yards and trailing hard. He saw her stumble, then stagger back to her feet only to stumble and fall again, still making progress, but if she wasn't coping with the relatively flat terrain there was no way she'd handle the challenge of the mountains. He wasn't even sure he'd be able to cope, never mind her.

When he reached the tent and bundles of bivouacs still lying beside it, he sank to his knees, grateful finally to have stopped moving.

He couldn't feel his fingers.

Bones clapped him on the shoulder then walked past him to help bring the girl into camp. The fall into the icy water had clearly taken far more out of him than he realized. How much more did he have to give?

ELEVEN

Morning came before the dawn, a peculiarity that would take some getting used to.

The hours had passed but there was still no sign of the sun. They had to press on regardless, even if the closest they had to light was the silver moon.

"Time to take the lie of the land, scout around out there, see what we're really up against," Maddock said.

"You feeling up to it, dude? You don't look too good." Bones replied. "I could cover for you, you rest up?"

"Just try and stop me." No matter what the big guy said, Maddock felt much better than he had any right to. Stiff, yes, his muscles tighter than they needed to be. His pigheadedness on the march might actually have done him some good. "Send a couple of the other guys to take a look over that peak there, we need an idea what's on the other side," he faced the mountains and waved an arm toward one of the shallower peaks. "We'll get one shot at this, and eyes are better than maps. We'll scout out this flank, between us we should get a decent eyes-on and find a line of least resistance through the range."

"With luck," Bones agreed.

"Better lucky than good," Maddock said.

"I'm coming with you." Leopov stumbled out of the tent. Barely awake, she was already fixing onto him like a second shadow.

"I don't know how you figure that one out," Maddock said. "We'll be quicker if it's just the two of us."

"I've got my orders..."

"OK, let me rephrase it. I'm in charge of this mission, and no matter what you think, I'm issuing you a field order that supersedes anything you've been told previously. You won't be able to keep up with us. That means you will jeopardize the effectiveness of the maneuver. That means it's not happening. Understood?"

Leopov looked skeptical. "How long?"

"A couple of hours, three tops. By then we should be ready to move on."

"Try not to miss me too much," Bones said with a wry smile.

She nodded as if giving her approval despite the fact Maddock hadn't asked for it, or needed it.

They struck out with little more than a mug of coffee in their bellies. Professor had started the primus stove and used melted snow to start a brew. Maddock had tasted better, but he'd drunk a lot worse. It provided a warm lining in his stomach, radiating heat through his body as they trudged along.

They walked in relative silence; this was about being vigilant, not just covering the distance.

Twenty minutes out of basecamp Bones stopped dead in his tracks.

"What the hell is that?" the big man asked, unslinging the rifle from his shoulder in readiness. Maddock followed his gaze. He saw the dark shape moving from the mountains. At first glance it looked like a bear moving toward them on its hind legs. They'd been warned about polar bears in the mission brief, but surely they were white rather than brown?

Bones already had an eye to the telescopic sight.

His finger poised over the trigger in case the object posed any kind of threat. The last thing they needed was a couple tons of polar bear charging at them.

"It's a man!" Bones offered the rifle to Maddock so he could take a look through the scope himself.

He was right.

It was a man.

As he grew closer his hood blew back from his face, revealing wild unkempt hair and a jet black beard. His arms gesticulated wildly toward them, but Maddock couldn't tell if it was a wave in welcome or warning, trying to drive them away. There were no obvious indications that the man was armed, but Maddock wasn't taking any chances. He kept the weapon trained on the newcomer until he came within earshot.

The man was babbling in Russian. Neither Maddock nor Bones could understand what the man was saying.

"Ironic how the one person who could help us out right now is the one person you didn't want out on the ice, eh chief?" Bones laugh held no mirth.

"I'd question your definition of irony." Maddock grimaced.

"He looks nuts to me. You think he's been out in this too long? This place is enough to drive anyone crazy if you're left on your own."

"I don't know. Why would he even be alone? Why would anyone want to be on their own in a place like this?" Maddock couldn't understand what this madman was doing out in the middle of this desolate island.

"Escaped from the gulag, maybe?"

"Possibly. In which case, he'll have a patrol on his heels." Maddock's stomach sank at the thought.

"Tell them to bring it," Bones said. "I'm ready to mess somebody up."

The man fell to his knees just a couple of yards away from them, seemingly repeating the same few sounds over and over again. They lost definition until it became utterly impossible to separate them, and mumbled into incoherence. Maddock thought he picked up one word, but he couldn't be sure. It didn't sound quite right to his ears, but that could have been down to the language barrier. "Romanov?" He said it out loud, seemingly not really knowing who he was talking to, or if he was just muttering to himself. He certainly didn't seem to be expecting a response.

"What about the Romanovs?" Bones asked.

"They were the last Russian royal family. He's saying, *'Romanov's Bane is lost,'*" a voice said behind him.

Maddock turned to find that Leopov had disobeyed his direct order and followed them after all. "I thought I'd told you to stay at the camp."

"Good thing I didn't listen to you then, isn't it?" She grinned and winked as she moved past Maddock and Bones.

The man on his knees still babbled on, showing no sign of stopping. His words grew ever more urgent. A wild madness ran rampant in his eyes. Leopov crouched down and spoke to him softly. Whatever she said seemed to calm him.

"What did you say to him?" Maddock asked.

"I just told him that he was safe."

"So what do we do with him?" Bones asked. "We can't just leave him out here can we?"

That was exactly what they ought to do, Maddock knew, but Bones was right. If they left him out here the risk was that the Russian team would stumble upon him. There was no way of knowing what he'd tell them, but Maddock didn't want the Spetsnaz boys knowing they had company out here on the ice if he could possibly help it. And if the Russians didn't stumble on him, the chances were the old man would be dead before too long; surely it wasn't possible to survive in a place like this alone without at least some form of support?

"We take him back," Maddock said. "We need to keep him with us for now at least. We don't need his death on our hands. He's done nothing to us. Besides, he might prove useful if the lieutenant can get through to him."

Bones leaned close to Maddock's ear and spoke softly. "This Romanov thing is weird. There are all kinds of mysteries and legends surrounding them."

"More of your unusual reading?" Maddock mumbled.

"I'm telling you, bro, something about this is all jacked-up."

Leopov spoke to the man again, placing one mittened hand on his shoulder. He nodded vigorously in response.

"I said that we'd give him something to eat and drink." Her level stare said she was committed to this course of action and would not be swayed.

Maddock had no choice but to trust her.

TWELVE

They settled the refugee inside one of the tents, and gave him a mug of steaming hot coffee and something to eat. His hands clutched the cup tightly. He held it close to his face, the warmth melting some of the frost that rimed his beard. He had fallen silent once they'd given him the food, his teeth snatching at it and gulping it down as quickly as he could. Every now and then he cast an eye at the others, fearful that they'd try and snatch it away from him. His eyes were still wild.

"He's not a local," Professor said as they stood outside the tent.

Maddock wasn't quite sure what he meant by it, but said nothing. He was more concerned about how long it was going to take for the second set of scouts to report back. Every moment that passed made him feel a little itchier.

"His features are inconsistent with the people who settled on the island," Professor continued. He fell into a comfortable—long—rambling speech about the Chukchi people who had settled Wrangel Island. Maddock switched off. Bitter experience had helped him develop a boredom filter; he knew the difference between the times when Professor had something interesting to say and the times when he merely trotted out something he'd learned along the way.

"Shaw and Lewis should have been back by now," Maddock said, breaking the spell Professor had worked hard to weave.

"Chill," Bones said. "Those two guys seem to know what they are doing."

Maddock checked his watch.

They'd been back for more than half an hour, and

even though their expedition had been cut short by the discovery of the wild man, it was still getting into the kind of time when they should have been able to see the guys returning across the ice at least. There was still no sign of them. It didn't necessarily mean something was wrong, but no matter how experienced the two of them might be, it was harsh out there. A mistake could prove fatal, and that wasn't even considering the Russians.

"We need to know who he is," he said at last.

There was still a mission on the table. And while there was no reason to imagine that the old man was part of it, he couldn't shake the sense that he was, somehow.

"Then Leopov needs to turn the thumbscrews," Bones said.

The words echoed Maddock's own thoughts. That was the reason the Lieutenant was here. Interaction. Translation. Time for her to start earning her keep. Use all the assets at your disposal, wasn't that what Maxey kept banging on about. He turned to finding that she was watching him. He tried offering a smile. It wasn't a natural look on him.

Leopov folded her arms across her chest, her gaze boring into Maddock. "So now you want my help?"

"Beggars can't be choosers," Maddock said.

"It's what I'm here for," she replied, echoing his thoughts.

He glanced down at his watch. It was creeping toward the three hour mark since they'd sent the scouts out. That wasn't good. They should have had eyes-on by now. They were going to have to go looking for the two scouts.

"Look. I'm sorry, okay? It's nothing personal."

"If you say so," she said, not exactly accepting the apology, as half-hearted as it was.

Maddock wasn't focused on her reply. "I'm going to have to take another walk on the ice," he said. "I would say you're welcome to join me, Zara," he said, deliberately using her first name for once. "But honestly, if those guys are in trouble out there I'm not sure what you can bring to the party."

She took a deep breath, biting down on the objection, and nodded. He was right.

"Give me some time and I'll have this guy's life story for you. Anything specific you're looking for?"

"You know the drill: where he's come from would be a good start, how he managed to get here. Anything else would be a bonus. Willis is keeping an eye on him. We'll leave him with you in case you need the extra muscle."

"I doubt I'll need him, but that's fine. Just leave it with me. Now go bring those boys home, Maddock, while I try to get some sense out of the Russian." She turned and headed inside the tent.

"You okay to take another walk?" Maddock asked Bones.

The Cherokee had been taking a load off by perching on the sledge. He was ready to move out in an instant. He had a single stretch of his limbs, arcing his back, then slung the rifle over his shoulder. "Good to go."

Maddock turned to Professor. "Professor, see if the ship's got a better fix on that location while we're away," he said. "We're losing time." He didn't need to say anything else.

"Sure thing," said Professor, and stealing a line straight out of Hill Street Blues, added, "Let's be careful out there."

No sooner had the words left his lips than Maddock heard the unmistakable report of a single gunshot, though it echoed and folded around the mountains, seeming to roll like thunder for seconds.

Though he didn't know who had fired it, or for what reason, in his gut Maddock feared that that gunshot would be heard all around the world.

THIRTEEN

It was almost impossible to be sure where the source of the gunshot lay, but they struck out in the direction they'd sent the scouts and trusted to luck. There wasn't a second gunshot to follow. Less than twenty minutes after leaving camp they spotted a dark shape against the white of the ice. It wasn't moving. Maddock increased the length of his stride. The heavy winter clothes and boots made running difficult, each lumbering step sinking through the crust of snow, each breath burning cold as he sucked it in, even at this 'easy' pace.

"Hey!" Maddock shouted as they started to approach, seeing not one body lying on the ground, but two. One of them lay atop the other, shielding the man on the ground with his own body. He heard no response to his call, so he tried again, "Shaw! Lewis!" Still nothing. No sound, no movement. Maddock turned the first body over, laying him down on the ice.

First thought, primary fear: that the man had been brought down by a Russian bullet. The reality was far worse.

It took a moment to be sure who he was looking at.

The man's throat and half of his face had been torn away, the flesh already freezing where it had been pared down to the bone and touched the ice. This wasn't something a man would have done, no matter how barbaric. Not even the Russians would do this to an enemy combatant. This was an animal's doing. The heavy coat had offered some protection, but it had not been enough. There was no sign of life. Maddock pulled the man's hood back to reveal a mop of red hair.

"Lewis," he said. Beside the dead man's body, the other SEAL gave a groan. He was still alive, barely, his companion's sacrifice having shielded him from the worst of the attack.

Maddock turned his attention to the living.

"Shaw, can you hear me?" He placed a hand on the other man's chest. Nate Shaw's lips were almost blue with cold, but they moved, breath escaping from between them in wisps and curls. He groaned. His eyes flickered open for a moment before closing again. He was coming around. Maddock checked him over. A deep gash in his arm poured blood. The material of his jacket was in shreds and stained with blood that had frozen into the lining, leaving it stiff and rigid.

"Come on, Shaw. Back to us. We've got a mission and we need you present." The man's eyes flickered again and he tried to lift his head. A minute or so later he was sitting upright clutching his arm and gritting chattering teeth. Maddock had no way of knowing how much damage he had done, tendon and ligament almost certainly, as he couldn't move it, but they wouldn't know for sure until they got him out of his gear.

If he could still walk it would be a bonus.

"How are you doing?"

Shaw moved his lips, unable to speak, but he could tell what the man was trying to ask: *Is Lewis okay?*

Maddock shook his head. He didn't need to say a word to convey his meaning. Nate was a SEAL. He knew exactly what that little gesture meant. Men die. It was the one unwritten rule of the job.

"What attacked you?"

Shaw managed a small shake of his head. Maddock decided against asking further questions. He looped an arm around the injured man's back and helped him to his feet. Nate Shaw sagged against him, scarcely able to remain upright.

Bones had his rifle at the ready, circling around to keep a lookout all around them. There was no other living thing as far as the eye could see, but something had done this to Shaw and Lewis. And it could return at any minute. Lewis had managed to get a shot off but there was very little blood that couldn't be accounted for from the savaging it had earned the dead man. They saw no sign of a dead animal out there, no trail of blood leading away from the body, but there were tracks in the ice and snow.

"What did this? A polar bear?" Maddock asked. He knew the big bears were the apex predators on Wrangel Island. Certainly neither the native wolves nor Arctic foxes could have done this.

"Big cat." Bones narrowed his eyes as he focused on the scene. "I can tell by the tracks." There was absolute confidence in the statement, even though Maddock hadn't seen the big man give the tracks any more than a cursory glance. "We need to move out."

Maddock didn't doubt him for a second, thought he was puzzled at the revelation. Big cats on Wrangel Island? That hadn't been part of the briefing. In any case, he wasn't about to argue. Bones' woodscraft was top-notch, so Maddock trusted him. Even so, Bones offered an explanation, "Just because the tracks lead away there's nothing to say that it traveled in a straight line. It's probably watching us, circling around just out of sight."

"We have to get you back to camp," Maddock said to Shaw. "And we can't leave Lewis out on the ice. If Russians don't find him some animal will. No one deserves that. He comes with us."

Bones handed over his rifle and Maddock accepted it.

The big man lifted the body from the ground and heaved it up over one shoulder. There was a respect about it even though he was carried him like a side of beef. Maddock held the rifle at the ready, eyes constantly darting left and right, checking all around them as they walked. Every now and then the pair exchanged the burden to spell the other man, but they were both relieved when the camp came into sight once more.

Two figures came running toward them as they approached, ready to take the burden of their fallen comrade. Nate Shaw was weakening fast. He needed to lean on Leopov, who held up under his weight and guided him back to the tent.

Our first casualty, Maddock thought, *and we haven't even met the Russians yet.*

FOURTEEN

Professor patched Shaw up as best he could under the circumstances. The gash was deep and had done bone damage that couldn't be dealt with here on the ice with basic field supplies.

"If we're lucky they'll have something on the submarine," Professor suggested, packing away the limited first aid kit they were carrying. He'd dressed the wound and given Shaw a morphine shot to dull the pain. He couldn't do any more than that.

"Then the sooner we get there the better," Maddock said. "We aren't going to find help anywhere else."

"What are we doing about Seb?" Shaw whispered.

"He comes with us," Maddock said. "The ice is too thick for us to break through to the ground and bury him without proper tools. Even if we built a snow bank and a stone cairn to cover him, we can't risk the Russians stumbling across his body. So we're taking him home."

Professor considered the implications of trying to get a corpse across the mountains. Maddock knew what was going through his mind. The order had just made the trek exponentially more difficult. But that didn't matter. No man was getting left behind. It wasn't happening.

"I'll strap him to the sledge," Bones said. "It'll mean redistributing supplies with everyone carrying more than before."

"Give Leopov and the Russian a pack if you need to. Shaw won't be taking one up the hill."

"I am here you know," Nate reminded them in a weak voice. "And I'm not going to let someone else carry my share. Don't worry about me. While I'm breathing, I'll be good."

They were on the move within the hour.

Maddock led the way with Leopov and the Russian behind him. Professor took first shift pulling the sledge. Nate Shaw had wanted to do it, but Maddock told him to wait his turn. They'd make it somehow. But they'd only make it if they did it together. It was as simple as that.

The lower slopes were frustratingly slow going despite the fact that there were narrow tracks through the ice. They began to crumble underfoot as the team made its way through the gullies and ravines and across the ridges of ice. Each obstacle became a feat of endurance and endeavor. Rocks and boulders rose through the ice, until the ground turned brown and started to show the first sign of spring.

"The mountains have their own microclimate," Professor said as they got the sled moving again. He was breathing hard after righting it once more.

"Not that you would notice." Bones looked around as if the very landscape affronted him. "Once it gets this cold it's basically just cold. Anything else is just fancy words to say even colder."

Professor was about to offer a riposte when he lost his footing. Shale slid beneath his boots. He reached out to prevent his fall, but the weight of the body on the sledge dragged him back down the incline a dozen steps before anyone could react to arrest his backward fall. Bones moved faster still, putting himself behind the sledge and what would have been a long way down for Professor.

"Take five," said Maddock. It wasn't worth pushing on. Fatigue was creeping in. Mistakes were happening. It came down to less haste, more speed. He needed them all with him. He took the respite to check in with Leopov and find out if she'd managed to find out anything about their Russian friend.

The wild man hadn't been happy to join them on the

trek through the mountains. Maddock didn't know if it was fear or just the knowledge they were going back the way he'd come. After all, that meant he knew exactly what they were heading toward.

"What's he got to say for himself?"

The Russian didn't even look up when Maddock approached. Someone had given him another mug of coffee. Caffeine seemed to be his drug of choice. All well and good if it kept him placated.

"Not a lot," Leopov said. "I thought I'd got him talking for a moment, but the gunshot spooked him. He clammed up after that."

Maddock glanced at the corpse that had been wrapped inside one of the bivouacs before being secured onto the sledge. "Couldn't be helped. Professor's worried the animals will still be able to smell the blood." It was a reasonable fear, even if the temperature was still below freezing. The light was already dying on them. They needed to make the most of it before they were forced to stop. He sat for a few minutes, catching his breath, before the urge to keep moving overcame his fatigue. "Let's kick on while we can." His voice echoed back at him from the mountainside, making his call to the others louder than he had intended it to be.

"You notice that?" asked Professor.

"What?"

"The silence. Apart from your voice there was nothing. Not even a roosting bird startled by the noise. Nothing. That's not natural. The world just isn't that quiet, even out here."

Maddock hadn't noticed.

He had been too caught up in thinking about what they should do next; how far they could make it before it was too dark to continue on safely. The ledge they were on was narrow, the crevasse it skirted deep. What had just happened to Professor was an abject reminder of what would happen if the sled went over the side. And what would happen to the man harnessed to it.

"We keep moving. If there's something out there then it's going to follow."

"What if it's herding us?" Willis asked.

"We'll cross that bridge when we come to it. Right now, let's keep things simple. Keep your eyes peeled, but don't fire a shot unless you *have* to. You heard Lewis' shot. That thing was heard miles away. I don't want us to make any more noise than we absolutely have to. The Russians aren't dumb. Spetsnaz are the best of the best they've got to offer. It could even be them on our trail, so let's make them work for it."

The others nodded.

They walked on into the night, gaining another couple of klicks before they had to concede defeat. The mountains were far more inhospitable than the ice had been. But, at least on this higher ground there were trees and kindling to make a fire. The wood was cold and damp, and drawing a blaze out of it was hard, but eventually Bones had a guttering fire that hissed and sparked. They were sheltered enough not to risk the flames being seen from a distance and the smoke rose into the darkness of the night sky unseen.

"We're never going to beat the Russians at this pace." Maddock knew they were all thinking it. They sat around the fire enjoying the heat radiating from it. Even the crazy Russian seemed to have finally calmed down, no more cries about Romanov's Bane. He stared into the flickering light, lost in thoughts he seemed unable to express. Maddock was happy to enjoy the silence.

"We could bury Lewis here," Professor suggested. "At least temporarily. Pick him up on the way back."

"The ground's solid, Prof. It's not happening." Bones didn't take his eyes from the fire.

"There's no need to dig. We just build a cairn."

Maddock knew that Professor was right. It made sense. They were going to be too slow dragging the sled along and taking the extra burden on their backs. It would be better to abandon it here and bury Lewis as best they could, protecting his body from scavengers until they could come back for him.

"All right, let's gather some rocks. Shaw, you sit this one out. Don't argue. That's an order."

Shaw nodded, relief evident on his face.

The rest fanned out, gathering large stones with which to protect their fallen comrade's body. It wasn't long before Maddock made a grisly discovery.

"Hey Bones," he called to Bonebrake, who stood nearby. "Take a look at this." The big man lumbered over to Maddock's side, stopping short when he saw what held Maddock's attention.

"What the hell? It can't be."

"I know," Maddock agreed, "yet here it is, and I think we can both agree it's fresh."

They knelt alongside the shredded carcass of a young mammoth. This one was young, though not a baby. It had stood four feet at the shoulder. The area all around showed the signs of its death struggle—mammoth prints, gouts of frozen blood and flesh… and the prints of big cats.

"I guess some small mammoth population survived on the island," Maddock said.

"No way," Bones said. "Word would have gotten out, or researchers would have found them." He took a deep breath and let it out in a rush. "I suppose anything's possible, but I'll bet you these are a relatively recent addition to the island."

"You mean someone rediscovered an existing population somewhere else? What, like Siberia?"

"Maybe. But science has been theorizing ways to bring back the mammoth for as long as I can remember. If someone found a well-preserved mammoth…" He lapsed into silence as the two of them stared at the carcass.

"I don't suppose it matters," Maddock finally said. "We've got the Russians to deal with and maybe these big cats as well. This is a mystery that can keep until later. For now, let's bury our friend."

FIFTEEN

Even the Russian helped to gather rocks.

It took more than an hour to build the cairn once they had settled the sledge and the corpse in a hollow in the hillside. Each stone was laid with care and precision, none of them wanting to inflict any harm on the man they were laying to rest. He was one of them, even if they hadn't known him as long or as well as the rest of the team. They took his loss personally and wanted the best resting place for him in case they didn't come back this way, which all of them knew to be a very real possibility even if they weren't voicing it.

At last they settled down in front of the fire to a meal prepared from the supplies they had brought with them. In the stillness of the night they ate in silence.

As if by unspoken agreement, neither Maddock nor Bones mentioned the dead mammoth. No need to cause alarm or to give the others a reason to wander off in the darkness. They already knew there might be one or more large predators following them, so the discovery of the recently-alive prehistoric pachyderm gave them no new information that would be useful in their current plight. So, they remained silent.

The fire crackled.

In the distance they could hear the hoot of an owl.

Maddock searched the night sky in the hope of catching sight of it even though he knew there was little chance of spotting a dark shape against the bruise-purple sky.

He was still searching the sky when he heard the sound of movement. He turned toward the sound, finger to his lips.

Bones' eyes narrowed. He had heard it, too. He sprang

to his feet, weapon in hand.

Maddock snatched up a torch and waved it in the direction of the sound, only to hear another faint crunch behind him. The torch *whickered* in the air as he turned quickly, light flashing on a pair of yellow eyes in the near black that were gone as quickly as they were seen.

"It was one of them." Nate Shaw lurched to his feet, fear ripe in his voice. Despite his injured arm he was immediately at Maddock's side, a broken branch blazing in his hand. It cut through the air leaving a trail behind as it moved.

"I thought you didn't see what hit you?" Maddock asked.

"I didn't *believe* it. I was sure it couldn't be something like that. Not here. I thought it was my mind playing tricks on me. There was no way I was going to let you all think I was crazy."

"Tiger, tiger, burning bright," Professor muttered under his breath as he snatched up another of the burning brands and waved it out in from of him, filling up the gaps in the circle until they all had the fire to their backs.

"What?" said Maddock.

"It was a tiger," Professor said. "But it wasn't like any kind of tiger I've seen before."

"Are you sure?"

"I'm sure." Professor gave him the briefest of glances as he swung the branch again. "And if I were a betting man, I'd slap few bucks on it being a sabertooth."

"A sabertoothed tiger? Are you kidding me, Professor?" Bones asked.

"That would explain what mauled the mammoth," Maddock said.

"Mauled mammoth? What are y'all going on about?" Willis stood, eyes wide, weapon at the ready.

"We found a mammoth carcass while we were gathering rocks." Maddock took a deep breath, eyes still searching the circle of darkness beyond the firelight. "A fresh kill."

"Unbelievable," Willis muttered.

Maddock caught sight of a beast's face as he swung the burning torch toward the darkness again. He saw it in fleeting glimpses, but that open mouth and huge incisors as it released a roar were unmistakable. Worse, the fire wasn't frightening it away. It barely held the creature at bay, and it wouldn't burn forever. Maddock switched the brand to his left hand and pulled out his pistol.

Before he could take aim Bones placed a hand on his arm.

He shook his head. "We can't kill something like this, Maddock. We don't have the right. They're the last of their kind, thought lost to mankind."

"What? It's kill or be killed," said Maddock, bluntly.

"I don't think so. Look at them. They aren't attacking us. It's the fire. They don't like it. As long as we keep it going, we ought to be okay."

Maddock wasn't convinced. "They seem too comfortable with it, if you ask me." There was no guarantee the wood would keep the fire burning until the sun rose. "What do you suggest?"

"We scare them off."

One of the sabertooths roared again, this time from somewhere on the slope above them. He looked up to see one of the great cats on a ledge no more than fifteen feet above their heads. Maddock turned to face it, holding his gun at the ready. Leopov stood closest to the creature. He understood why Bones wouldn't want to kill it. Yes, it was beautiful even if it was dangerous. Yes, it should by rights have been extinct, but it was a clear and present threat. He hesitated for a heartbeat too long. The beast leaped toward them, its great paws the size of a man's head, lethal claws extended, ready to tear out his throat given half a chance.

He'd seen what one of these things had done to Seb

Lewis. He wasn't going the same way. Acting on instinct and ingrained training as opposed to deliberate thought, he pushed Leopov to one side, putting himself between her and them.

The great cat landed where the woman had been standing a fraction of a second before, a couple of feet from the roaring fire. Its feet slithered in grit and gravel as it clawed at the ice bank in a desperate attempt to keep its footing. It threw back its immense head and loosed another peak-rattling roar.

Maddock fired into the air, hoping that the shock of the noise would be enough to scare it away.

It wasn't.

The beast paused for a moment but made no sign of turning tail.

Those few timeless seconds were enough for Maddock to snatch up the branch Leopov had been holding. Two blazing torches in hand he stood between her and the sabertooth. Desperate times called for desperate measures. Rather than holding back, he took a step forward slashing out with the brands. The flame rippled through the air in front of him. One step. Two steps. Closer.

He thrust the burning wood right into the creature's face.

It let out a howl of pain and shied away.

Maddock didn't give it a chance to overcome its fear.

He threw himself at it, the flame scorching the animal's fur. He lashed out again, catching it on the side of the face, going for the whiskers in the hope that it was as dependent upon them for balance as a modern feline. The sabertooth howled again, matching his wild slash with one from its

great paw. The big cat moved back and back, spine arched, fur on end, until it was pushed up against the hillside.

Fight or flight?

Cornered, it would likely be at its most dangerous.

Another flame appeared by Maddock's side. It was Leopov, two brands burning bright in her fists. The cat cowered, turning its head away from the heat for a moment, then bolted. Its howls faded away as it disappeared into the night.

"They've all gone," Bones said. No one broke from the defensive ring.

"You sure?"

"Sure," Professor agreed.

"I'll tell you who else has gone," Leopov said. The men all turned to look at her. "The Russian."

SIXTEEN

They let Leopov slip into the tent with some of the supplies and the radio pack.

Maddock knew that the men would get some respite from the cold once they were zipped into their bivouacs. Her job was to listen in on the radio for any kind of chatter from the Russians. He hated that they were blind. He wanted to know where the Spetsnaz team was with pinpoint accuracy. He didn't want them wiping their noses without him knowing about it. She'd picked up a fragment, but all she had been able to make out was the word *Pandora*. That had been enough to convince him their intelligence was correct.

The signal had come from a short wave radio. That meant they couldn't be too far away. There was no way of knowing who was broadcasting, but if it was the Spetsnaz team it meant they were no more than a matter of hours away, and possibly a lot less.

He waited until the others had settled down for a couple of hours sleep with their bellies full before he took Bones to one side. He didn't want there to be any risk of Leopov overhearing what he had to say.

"Are you still up for this?" Bones asked before Maddock had the chance to voice what was on his mind.

"Don't worry about me." He was not sure whether he was lying to Bones or to himself. He felt stronger now he'd eaten, but that didn't mean that he wasn't still carrying some of the aftereffects of his dunking.

"Okay, so what do you want to tell me?"

"The girl. She's not going to be able to keep up on any kind of forced march. If we don't have the Russian to worry about we should just push on. I'd rather not have to worry about her keeping up."

"This again?" Bones scowled. "Come on, Maddock. She's kept up so far. Don't you think she's proved herself?"

"She's going to hold us back," Maddock insisted.

"I don't know, man. What do you have in mind?"

"We leave her behind."

Bones gaped. "Leave her? Out here? Alone? After what just happened with the sabertooths? Are you out of your freaking mind? Hypothermia can mess with your brain, I guess, but seriously, dude, that's uncool in the extreme. We can't do that. I don't care how you dress it up."

"We don't have to leave her on her own. We push on and the others can hang back with her. At least that way we won't have to worry about her until this is done with."

Bones shook his head. "We don't break the team up. Rule one. Besides, she'll never go for it."

"I wasn't planning to give her a choice."

"What's really going on here, Maddock?" Bones fixed him with a knowing grin. "You got a thing for her?"

"No, I don't have thing." Privately, he wasn't so sure. The physical attraction was undeniable. Other than that, he didn't really know Leopov all that well, but he certainly felt something. "I just don't think she'll be safe where we're headed."

"I doubt it will work, bro. You saw what happened the last time you tried to leave her behind."

"We don't tell her. We get a couple of hours shut eye then we move on. The others can follow when they've rested. You and me, we could get across the mountains much faster if we don't have to worry about her. You know it and I know it. If we leave the packs we'll make double time."

"Just the two of us? You make it sound easy. I don't plan on being Oates to your Scott, man."

The reference to the famed polar explorers surprised Maddock. Not for the first time, he updated his assessment of Bones' intelligence and breadth of knowledge.

"That's fine, I don't intend on it, either." Maddock's mind was made up.

"So leave her here with the prehistoric predators?"

"Not alone. The rest of the crew will be here. We'll put Professor in charge. He'll be able to get the rest to the other side and find us. We get there first and at least get the chance to assess the situation even if we can't do anything without them. If the Russians are there, we get the chance to turn back without this turning into an international incident."

"Who are you trying to convince? And there was me thinking you and Leopov were going to get your freak on after your heroics back there."

"Think of it as a rush of blood to the head."

"Which one?"Bones waggled his eyebrows.

"Just for that, you can break it to Professor." Maddock said. "And the sooner you get it over with the better."

Professor took the news better than Maddock had expected. It was all about the mission. Sending a couple of scouts ahead made a lot of sense, as did keeping the woman back from the front line. He came to find Maddock.

"Take these." Professor handed over the GPS locator and the map.

"How will you manage?"

"I've already sketched a copy. I can manage not to get lost from here," he jabbed at the point where the two pencil lines crossed. "All I need's my trusty compass."

"What happens if the ship gives new coordinates?"

"Then I adjust and you have to wait for us to catch up. Either way, that's the point that I'll get the others to. How much of a head start do you need?"

"We're going to grab a couple of hours shut eye, then we're striking out. Give us at least an hour's start before you break camp. That should be enough to keep Leopov from chasing us."

Maddock hoped his instincts were right about this.

SEVENTEEN

Maddock's internal alarm clock woke him after a few short hours. Nearby, he saw Bones stirring.

"Morning," Bones grunted. It wasn't exactly the wake-up call dreams were made of. Bones just wasn't pretty enough for that.

Maddock mumbled a reply that wasn't exactly full of rise-and-shine. He stretched inside the confines of the bivouac. It took a moment to gather his senses. He felt bone tired. Sleeping on the hard ground hadn't helped. But he was dry and warm and his blood hadn't frozen in his veins overnight. That was a win. The drawstring pulled the opening of the bag tight around his face so that only the smallest part of him was exposed to the open air, and even that was partly covered by a scarf. He tugged at the string to release the fastening and started to wriggle free from the cocoon. Two minutes later he was ready to roll out.

Professor was awake. He said nothing; just gave them a nod from inside his bag and closed his eyes again without a word.

Bones pulled a heavy pack up onto his back. Maddock moved to do likewise, but the big man shook his head and made a 'just the one' gesture with his finger. They had all they needed in the one pack to make it through a day or so on the ice, no point making it more of a burden than it needed to be. Maddock nodded. Professor could handle distribution of the stuff he left behind. It didn't look as though the Cherokee had slept. His sheer levels of endurance were staggering. He was like the Energizer Bunny: he could go on and on and on. Of course it helped that he hadn't plunged into icy water and nearly frozen himself to death. It felt like days had passed since it had happened to him.

They walked in silence for more than a hundred yards before either of them said a word.

"You think she's going to be pissed when she finds out what you've done?"

"Yep." Maddock glanced back, relieved to see no movement in the camp.

He hoped that Professor had settled back to sleep for another hour or two. They would need as much rest as possible before they carried on. An hour snatched here, another hour snatched there, was no good, not really. The conditions were so much more demanding than a simple trek. "I'd expect nothing less." But he wasn't going to worry about her for a while. She'd get her chance to bitch and moan once they were back together, job done. It was much harder to complain about a decision when it had been proven to be the right one. Her orders didn't matter. The mission objectives did. It was as simple as that. Her lords and masters were the ones who'd screwed her up by putting her in in a situation she wasn't equipped to handle.

The ground started to rise sharply as they climbed, the going becoming progressively more difficult with every few steps they took. The moon provided sufficient light for them to see the sparkle of the ice, a warning that a misplaced step could send them sliding down the mountainside. In an ideal world they would have had satellite images to guide them through this terrain. They had only an outdated map that Professor had given them. Still, it was better than nothing.

In places they fell beneath the shadows of crags and overhangs, and needed a flashlight to increase visibility. He kept a hand over the beam, hooding it. He didn't want to broadcast their position.

It felt good to be moving though, good to be setting himself against nature and proving himself again. Mainly, though, it was good to prove to himself that yesterday's accident had caused no lasting effect. It could have been a lot worse.

As they emerged from the shadows, he turned the flashlight off, relying once again on no more than the moonlight.

Catching them unawares the land seemed to flatten out in front of them, stretching out for as far as the eye could see. All that lay ahead of them was the whiteness of the ice and the deep blue black of the night sky. Maddock checked the GPS signal to make sure of their bearings, then struck out again, quickening their pace until their steps began to eat up the yards, the exertion keeping the cold at bay. By the time they reached the far edge of the ice sheet the sky had grown lighter. The others would be moving by now, but they were far enough ahead not to worry about being caught.

On and on the ice went.

What had been easy became hard as the wind picked up, swirling loose snow up into their faces, sucking the heat out of their lungs. What had been hard became impossible as the wind drove into their faces, cutting them down to size. They were insignificant specks. They were motes in the eye of the storm. They were struggling. Each step became more labored than the last. Maddock drove himself on. Bones trudged beside him, hating every minute of it.

At last, as they picked their way back down toward sea level, he knew that they must be getting close to the point Professor had picked out on the map. He'd hoped that there would be more glimpses of blue amongst the white, but the ice was packed tighter here than it had been where they'd left the ship. The GPS confirmed that they were getting close. Maddock pulled out his binoculars and adjusted the magnification, scanning the horizon, looking for a shape that was out of place. Even with the adjustment, the one thing he saw was too far away to be able to be absolutely sure of its nature, but if he'd had to bet his life on it, he'd have said that spur jutting up out of the ice was the conning tower of a submarine. He passed the binoculars to Bones and pointed to where he should be looking.

"Well, well, well, what have we got here then?" Bones scanned the white before focusing on the stark black streak of the sub piercing up through the surface, and the spill-back of ice that trapped it.

Maddock looked up at the sky. It was day now, but for how much longer in this strange land of night and more night? They had an hour, two, maybe three before full night settled in again, but how long before daylight too quickly began to fade? They needed to move, take advantage of the daylight. He ran the numbers in his head. The others should have broken camp and be on the trail behind them, but moving slower, so maybe three or four hours behind them. Time made all the difference now. Even minutes. He had no idea what they were likely to find when they reached the *Echo II*. The crew could all be dead, or too sick to help themselves, they could be ready to fire on anyone who approached keeping some sort of self-imposed quarantine, knowing that whatever was killing them had to die out here on the ice with them, or, worst of the four possibilities, the Spetsnaz team could have already beaten them to the punch.

"Someone following us." Bones turned a hundred and eighty degrees. He swept the landscape with the binocular lenses. "I can't see them, but they're there, I'm sure of it."

Maddock had had the same feeling for the last couple of klicks, but whenever he'd glanced back over his shoulder to check there'd been no sign of anyone back there. "A saber tooth tracking us?"

"Maybe," Bones shrugged. "Stealthy enough, for sure. I can't seem to get more than a glimpse of a shadow-shape in my peripheral vision, gone before I can focus on it. But it could be the Russian."

"You think he's still out there? I'd be amazed if he's even alive, those cats would have him, surely, easy pickings?"

"Stranger things happen, man," said Bones. "He's survived this long."

"Let's just hope that whoever it is keeps their distance until this is all over."

They walked on, focused on the conning tower.

The ice grew more uneven as they ventured further out onto it. Initially, it was just ripples and ridges in the plate that made the ground uncertain, but the ridges grew into ice dunes the further they walked. The dunes were more challenging to cross as the surface around them revealed fissures where the impacted ice, forced up to form those dunes, stretched thin. Some of those dunes and ridges rose above head height on either side of them. As they walked, Maddock could feel the sheer relentless weight of the ice pressing in all around them. It was claustrophobic. The sheets of ice had compacted against each other, the pressure of more ice creeping out from the shore pushing hard behind it. The only way it could escape that relentless pressure was up. And something would have to give then. Gravity would not be placated for long, even as the ice formed huge glacial drips and frozen waterfalls all around them as they ventured off solid ground onto an ice platform suspended above the sea. It creaked and groaned under the shifting pressure.

Maddock wanted off the ice as quickly as possible, knowing better than anyone what lay beneath.

EIGHTEEN

The ice flattened out.

It was young, not yet pushed, cracked and splintered under the pressure of the next sheet forming behind it.

It also meant that the surface was thinner in patches and less secure.

Closer now, there was no mistaking the submarine's conning tower. The sub had been pushed up in the ice, the prow protruding from the ice at an angle, the sail still clear of the surface. It was obvious that nothing the crew attempted would have liberated it from the ice, but equally there was nothing to stop them from climbing out and striking out across the frozen landscape in search of what passed for civilization on Wrangel Island. The Spetsnaz team couldn't be far away, but there was no sign of them. He didn't think they were too late, because the snow around the sub appeared undisturbed by anything apart from the wind.

"You know this thing could be the death of us, don't you?" Bones asked as they quickened their pace. Neither one of them had to say they needed to push on.

"The ice? The radiation or whatever it is that has been released inside that sub?" Maddock asked. "Or do you just mean the Russians?"

"All three." Bones replied. "But you knew that, didn't you? That's why you made the others stay behind. It's never been about speed for you, has it? This was only ever going to take two of us if we actually made it this far. We both know that there's a sickness on board and that the crew won't be fighting back."

"If there's anyone still alive." Maddock still harbored grim hopes there might be some survivors to help without compromising the mission, but the last shreds of that hope were slipping away. He didn't expect to find anyone alive. Yes, the Russian had come from somewhere, but not the sub. He was either a native, or an escapee from the Gulag.

They covered the last klick in silence. Each step took them further out onto the frozen sea. The ice held the submarine in a vice like grip. The paused for a moment before they stepped into the shadow of the great vessel, dwarfed by the conning tower and the bulwark spearing out of the ice like a torpedo trapped mid-launch, frozen in time and ice. Maddock was lost in thought. It took a moment for the strangely familiar *click, click click* to fight its way through his subconscious to the front of his mind. He turned to face Bones.

The big man had a Geiger counter in his hand.

"Radiation," he said matter-of-factly. "We don't want to be hanging around here longer than we absolutely need to. And even that's going to be too long *inside* there. The level's not dangerous out here, but it's bad enough. If we're going to do this, we'd better get it over with."

Maddock nodded. No choice. The objective was clear. Retrieve Pandora's Egg. Whatever the hell Pandora's Egg was.

A sheen of ice coated the metal. There were enough ridges and rivets to provide hand and foot holds, but it wouldn't make an easy climb. They had to move with care, knowing that every footfall would sound like a hammer within the sub, announcing their arrival to anyone not too dead to hear it. They climbed until they stood beside the periscope atop the conning tower, and looked back down at the ice below.

It was a long dizzying drop.

"Well at least one of them came out this way." Bones pointed at the hatch. A metal bar had been wedged into the mechanism ensuring that no one on the inside would be able to get out.

He gave the bulges on either side of the submarine a cursory glance. He knew that was where the ICBMs were housed, already loaded into their launchers. The launchers were hidden behind hatches. There was no way in or out of the vessel that way.

Anyone still alive inside knew that visitors would have to come in through the front door.

NINETEEN

The interior of the sub lay in near darkness.

The only light came from the faint glow of instrument panels and emergency lighting. Maddock had been inside spaces like this both above and below the waterline. It was suffocating, but livable if you ignored the thought of just how little realistically separated you from the water. He knew his way around, basically, because the layout was going to be similar from submarine to submarine. He broke a glo-stick and dropped it down to the bottom of the ladder. It clattered down the rungs to the steel floor.

Nothing could have prepared him for what the light revealed.

At first he thought that the Russians were waiting for them, gathered together at the bottom, ready to take them as soon as they descended, but none of them moved or reacted to the light. They had died waiting to be rescued. Trapped inside by the metal bar jammed into the lock. Someone had passed judgment on them.

Did that mean they'd been beaten here?

"Looks like they froze to death," Bones said, first down the ladder.

It was hard not to step on a body as he reached the bottom. The crew had huddled up around the ladder, dressed for the outside in full winter gear, with mittens and ski masks beneath their hoods. It was as cold in here as it was out on the ice. Colder if anything.

"What about the illness? Radiation sickness?"

"Who knows? But this can't be *all* of the crew."

"How's the counter looking?" The moment Bones turned the device, he was greeted by clicks coming thick and fast. It was worse than outside. Not unexpected, but not good either. The reactor was obviously the source of the radioactivity, and given the readings weren't off the scale that meant it had to be shielded to some extent. But for how much longer? The submarine was not designed to take the stresses and strains of being trapped like this. Surely the integrity of the hull was at risk?

Maddock managed to find enough floor space to place a foot down, then carefully looked for another, using handholds overhead to pull himself through the mass of corpses. The deck inclined fairly steeply. He took the climb slowly, not wanting to stumble and fall into the pack of bodies.

The glow from an instrument panel lit up the frozen faces of crew still sitting in their seats.

There was no one here to save.

He tried not to think about the horror of it; dying trapped in a place like this, locked in a sardine can that slowly froze them.

"That sucks," Bones grunted, ever succinct. He wasn't wrong. That's exactly what they were."

"Let's get this over with, man," Maddock said. "The sooner we can get out of here the better." Bones didn't argue with him. It was all about finding Pandora's Egg.

Maddock moved slowly to the front of the submarine, climbing higher with each step. Metal groaned against metal with every movement, echoing with the relentless press of the ice on the hull. The *Echo II* had been built to sustain immense pressure at great depths, but this was different. How much more could it take before the stresses and strains were too much for it to bear and the great boat started to come apart at the seams? Would it be torn apart with them still inside it? What would happen to the shields around the reactor? How much damage would they be looking at if the core was breached? Would they even be safe if they made it back to the ship? Or was the entire island and every one on it already damned?

TWENTY

A grim scene like something out of a disaster movie lay before them.

There were bodies with sheets pulled over their heads strapped to bunks in the first three of the sections that Maddock checked. They hadn't begun to stink, the extreme cold trapped within the sub effectively refrigerating the dead. It was the smallest of mercies. He glanced at the faces. He wouldn't remember them. There were no clues as to what had killed them save for a faint yellowness around one of the dead submariner's lips. It wasn't much, and didn't discount any pathogen being airborne, or poison being tracked back to any surface that he came into contact with... if there was even a contagion... a poison...

The clock was ticking.

He moved through the sub, footsteps echoing as he ventured forward. The long galley, cramped and narrow, contained the smallest working surface he'd ever seen. It was miraculous that food emerged from it. The tiny dining area on the far side revealed the effects of the trauma that had happened onboard. There were a pair of tables that sat eight men and chairs secured in place, but the floor was littered with broken plates, cutlery, and scraps of food.

Was this what the end looked like?

It was a sobering thought—one day, maybe a day like today, one of these places would be his end. It was never as you imaged it, he knew that much. Never as heroic, normally commonplace and tragic. This was different on so many levels, and so much more horrific for it. This was drawn out, tortuous. Had they turned on each other at the end? Fought over scraps, desperate to survive a few hours more just in case help did arrive? He had no way of knowing, but it felt as though the last few days of their lives these men hadn't been living, or even just surviving, they'd been slowly dying.

He moved on, climbing gradually higher as he followed the rise of the sub where it was trapped trying to break through the ice.

One room was different from all of the others.

A man sat on the bunk in the corner, his back pressed against the bulkhead. For a moment Maddock thought he was still alive. He raised his pistol instinctively, drawing down on the corpse on the bed. There was a small pillow behind his head and blood on the walls around it. Maddock let out a long slow breath, but didn't take the gun off the man until he was absolutely sure he was dead. He played the flashlight around the cramped room for a moment. Unlike the others where the roll-on roll-off bunks were stacked three high, nine to a chamber no more than eight feet by eight, there was only one bed in here, meaning he was face-to-face with the captain. He'd blown his brains out. The blood was a dark smear on the wall behind him, fused around his hair and scalp, keeping him upright. He'd known that help wasn't coming and hadn't wanted to drag it out. Maddock couldn't understand that. In his philosophy hope was the last thing to die, not the first, even in a hellhole like this.

He stepped inside the comparatively spacious room. The door slammed behind him and bounced back open, the resonant clang echoing through the silence of the coffin. He heard a voice calling. Unless the dead had found a speaker, it had to be Bones.

"In here," he called back into the passageway, his voice sounding every bit as metallic as its surroundings as it filled the space. "I've found it."

He waited for a moment before he approached the captain's corpse, hearing Bones' footsteps approach.

Not in his wildest dreams had he expected that

Pandora's Egg could be as *beautiful* as this. It was a work of art, of supreme craftsmanship, a testament to the mastery of its creator.

"What have we got?" Bones asked as he stood in the doorway.

Maddock played the light over the dead man's hands. He slipped his gun back into its sheath, then took another step forward, reaching out for the object the man had clung onto even as he blew his own brains out, as if it was the most valuable thing in the world. And looking at it, maybe it was. Maddock had seen pictures of these things, who hadn't? But pictures couldn't hope to live up to the reality of one of the jewel encrusted eggs created by Fabergé for the Russian royal family. The Romanov's.

"Romanov's Bane," he breathed. "Isn't that what the Russian said?"

"I thought this thing was supposed to be a weapon?" asked Bones.

"Pandora's *Egg*. We haven't found anything else that fits the bill and it's too big a coincidence for it to be anything else. This has to be it." Maddock took the object from the ice cold hand of the dead man. "Which means that assuming our intel is right, it has to be a weapon." The body shifted in its final resting place as he took it, as if the man was reluctant to let it go, even in death.

"And worth a couple of bucks by the looks of it." Bones eyed the egg with admiration.

"Understatement of the year." Maddock turned the egg over in his mittened hands, noting the way the faint light danced along the surface of the gold filigree and patterned rubies and emeralds. The craftsmanship was exquisite. But his admiration for the beauty of the piece was overwhelmed by the knowledge that he held a rare and important piece of history in his hands.

"Well, assuming you're right, we need to get out of here, and scupper this thing if we can."

There was a dull rumble as he said it, almost as if the submarine was listening to him and voicing its objection to the idea. Maddock stood motionless for a moment as they both listened. The noise came through the hull, tortuous, anguished, as if the ice were losing its grip and the submarine was about to slip back into the water.

No. That was only part of it.

The sounds weren't just coming from outside the vessel and the shifting in the ice.

They were coming from inside.

For a heartbeat, less, Maddock thought the dead had risen as the dull clang of footsteps haunted them, then the door swung open.

Maddock turned, Pandora's Egg in his hands, to see Professor standing in the doorway. An unseen figure held a gun pressed against his temple.

TWENTY ONE

"Now, that wasn't so difficult, was it?" the man holding the gun said.

Maddock cursed the fact that the Spetsnaz agents, for that's who they had to be, were able to get on board in virtual silence. He'd heard they were good, but *this* good? He'd underestimated them. They must have been out on the ice at the same time, and yet he'd missed them in their white arctic camouflage gear. Maddock and Bones might have won the race to the sub, but the odds of them getting out with the prize were slim.

"Do the smart thing, gentlemen, drop your weapons on the floor and kick them under the captain's bunk." The Spetsnaz man's English was flawless. Better than flawless, it carried the faintest trace of a Boston accent. He'd heard about these spy schools the Russians had where they trained their men endlessly, churning out faux-Americans, sleeper agents capable of blending in perfectly until it was time for them to wake up. The Russian pressed the muzzle harder against Professor's head to reinforce the point.

Bones put his gun on the ground as another of the Spetsnaz operatives eased inside the now cramped chamber to pat each of them down. Maddock kicked his automatic under the bunk as instructed. He didn't relinquish his hold on the Egg. It wasn't as if he could palm it though. He wasn't exactly David Copperfield. The Russian pushed Professor inside with a savage shove that sent him stumbling against Bones. Professor's hands were tied behind his back. He saw Willis, grim-faced, in the corridor behind Professor.

"Sorry." Professor could have been apologizing for his clumsiness, for leading the Russians to the submarine or for telling them something under duress that the rest of the team wouldn't have the luxury of living to regret. It didn't matter now.

When the familiar face of the wild Russian they'd found on the ice appeared behind them in the doorway Maddock knew exactly how the Spetsnaz team had learned about their presence on the ice.

"I'll take that," he said, wrestling the egg from Maddock's hands.

Maddock didn't give it up easily, making the man struggle until the Spetsnaz operative cuffed him around the temple with the butt of his pistol. His fingers sprang open as if unlocked. And with that, any illusion of control passed completely to the Russians. He saw another one of them in the doorway, keeping Nate Shaw upright. The man looked like he was in a bad way. The sabertooth must have done more damage than he'd feared. It was obvious he needed proper medical attention and he wasn't likely to get it here. This was a place of death. Right now it reeked of it.

There was no doubting what the Russians intended. Maddock and his team were facing execution, yet he felt strangely calm.

The Spetsnaz team leader stepped back into the incline of the corridor and motioned with his gun for them to follow him out into the passage. There were too many of them to fight and no room in which to fight them. Maddock scanned the faces looking for Leopov, either as a prisoner or traitor. There was no sign of her. She'd been cozy with the mad Russian. Was she the one who'd betrayed them or was she lying dead on the ice somewhere?

With at least two weapons trained on each of them they had little choice but to do as they were told. They made their way back through the body of the submarine, but instead of stopping and being herded back up the ladder they were taken further along, crossing a narrow gantry beneath which the reactor itself was slowly leaking. One of the Spetsnaz operatives waited for them on the other side of the bridge that traversed the reactor. Maddock could still hear the dull hum of it beneath them, very much alive. He felt his skin crawl and knew it was purely psychological, but that didn't change just how creepy it was to be so close to so much raw power, like walking over a very small sun. The Russian swung open a door and stepped aside.

Maddock had to duck down to enter. He helped Shaw who collapsed against him as they stepped through. The man was unable to support his own weight. Willis had obviously worn himself out being Shaw's pillar of strength, but he was clearly close to exhaustion himself.

It was dark inside, but not fully black because of the dim glow from the emergency lighting that lined the bulkhead.

They were in the engine room. Where it should have been up over the hundred-degrees mark in the biggest room on the sub, the temperature was even colder because they were below the water line and no amount of insulation was enough to keep this part of the boat warm now the engine wasn't running. By rights, it should have been deafening too, but instead was eerily quiet.

Maddock scanned the engine room looking for anything that might help them.

There was no other way out, but that wasn't the biggest problem facing them. He saw a row of explosive charges had been fixed on the bulkhead, the Russians intending to scupper it themselves so nothing on here could fall into enemy hands.

"Feel free to try and disarm the explosives, obviously. It'll give you something to do while you wait to die. It won't help, but it is always good to at least feel like you have chance, isn't it?" the Spetsnaz officer said. He almost sounded friendly, like a guy in a bar discussing the Red

Sox. "But don't feel like you're missing out. Once that western lackey Gorbachev has opened his gift, things will be very different in the world. You wouldn't want to be around for it, believe me."

The door slammed closed behind them and the loss of the limited light from the corridor seemed to throw the engine room into absolute darkness even though the glow of the emergency lighting should have been enough for them to see by.

"Not exactly going according to plan," Bones observed.

"You think?" Maddock said.

"Unless the plan was to have defeat snatched from the jaws of victory?"

Maddock knew what he was doing—gallows humor. It was important in their way of life, laughing in the face of death.

"If those blow, this place is going to fill with water faster than you can say, *'We're screwed.'* The extra weight ought to free us from the ice and suck the sub under, but we won't be around to swim for freedom."

"Thanks for the motivational pep talk, Professor," said Bones. "You want to take a look, see if you can figure out how long we've got before it blows? Or, you know, if there's any way of stopping it?"

"What happened to Leopov?" Maddock asked.

"She must have slipped away not long after you left," Willis said. "We didn't notice until we started to break camp an hour or so after you'd gone. She'd already given us the slip by then."

"You think she went straight to the Russians?"

Professor shrugged. "I don't know. She wasn't with them when they picked us up."

There had to be another reason for her setting out on her own. He didn't want to believe he'd been suckered by a traitor. So until there was no other choice he was going to give her the benefit of the doubt. That meant she was out there, an unknown variable. They needed all the help they could get.

"There's a fifteen minute delay on those charges. You want me to pull them?" Professor told him.

"Not yet," said Maddock. "Keep an eye on the clock. One question: if that bulkhead blows do you think we'd have *any* chance of getting out that way?"

"Nope. Even if we did survive the blast, we'd never be able to fight our way through the water coming in. We'd have to wait until the engine room is almost full of seawater before we could strike out, and we'd have frozen to death by then."

"Right," Maddock said. "Why fifteen minutes?"

"Distance. If the entire ice shelf collapses when the sub blows they're giving themselves a fighting chance to get away" said Bones.

"They've got Skidoos," said Willis. "That's how they managed to get us here. I doubt Shaw would have made it here without them." Shaw sat on the floor, propped up against a control unit. He didn't look good. His face was white, leeched of all color. His lips were tinged with blue and his eyes looked murky. He needed help faster than they could get it for him. Then again, none of them had a life expectancy beyond quarter of an hour, so he'd live as long as any of them.

"Professor, do you think you could blow the door with one of those charges without setting the rest off?" Maddock asked.

"Doable." Professor gave the door no more than a cursory glance before answering.

"OK. Let's do it. Like our Russian friend said, why not go out fighting? I think he'd be disappointed if we didn't at least try."

Even as he said it his words were interrupted by a dulcet *clang* that echoed through the boat.

Maddock knew that sound: The hatch was being closed.

The Russians had left.

They wouldn't be coming back even if they heard the sound of all hell breaking loose inside the submarine. They only had fourteen minutes to clear the ice.

TWENTY TWO

Professor cursed under his breath.

"Problem?" Maddock asked.

"You know it. Moving the one charge has just wiped five minutes off the timer for the rest of the charges. I guess that's what he meant by not helping ourselves. Just get back from the door, I'll get this off its hinges."

Even with hands pressed tightly over his ears the blast thundered inside Maddock's head. It felt as if his brain had suddenly become too large for his skull. He wanted to scream against it for long seconds after his brain stopped rattling against the bone plates encasing it.

The door was still closed, but Professor was on his feet and pushing it open on the deserted corridor beyond. It crashed on the wire-grille floor. Maddock hauled himself to his feet, helping Bones to lift Shaw. Nate didn't look good, bringing his head up slowly. "I'm tired, man. Just… leave me here. You go, get out." Maddock could see the life gently ebbing away from the SEAL.

"We're not leaving you," Maddock said.

Shaw fixed him with a level gaze. "Even if you get me off this thing, you'll never get me back to the ship. I'll just hold you back."

"Yes we will," Maddock agreed. "And we'll do it because you're one of us." He started to drag-carry him toward the door. The man was a dead weight even with two of them trying to move him. He grunted in pain with every step, face twisting as he fought not to let it show.

"When those charges blow it's not going to take long for the engine room to fill," Professor said.

Maddock knew what the man was saying. If they didn't get out of there quickly, none of them would. He wanted all of them out. But he couldn't force them to all move at the pace of the slowest man. That would be murder.

"Go on ahead," he said to the others. "Get the hatch open and get out of here. Get as far as you can across the ice. Don't stop. Don't turn around. Don't look back. Just keep running. That's an order. Even you, Bones."

They didn't need to be told twice, even though Bones was clearly reluctant to leave Maddock and the dying man.

"We won't be far behind you," Maddock promised.

He didn't say any more than that. He knew that Bones didn't believe him. But the big Cherokee also knew that at least one of them had to survive to make sure the mission was completed. He was pragmatic. This was Maddock's choice. He respected that. Rolls reversed, Maddock liked to think he'd afford his friend the same respect, but he wasn't sure he could.

Boots clattered as the men ran up the incline, covering the distance as quickly as they could. Maddock watched them fade into the gloom of the poorly lit corridor.

They limped on.

"Seriously, Maddock. Go. I'm done. Get out. It's senseless both of us dying here. I appreciate what you're trying to do, but you're an idiot," Shaw said.

"It's my call," Maddock told him.

Shaw had to rest twice before they'd crossed the wire-grille bridge over the reactor. There was no way he was going to make it to the conning tower and the hatch.

Maddock didn't hurry him.

They moved slowly back to the galley where Bones waited in the doorway.

Maddock stared to yell at him, but Bones shook his head.

"It's not dumb loyalty, Maddock. No one is getting off this boat. We should have done a better job getting rid of that metal bar. The Russians haven't taken any chances. They've locked us in here. We're going down with the sub, and our one hope is getting out through the blast hole when those charges go off."

They both knew that their core temperatures would fall too low for them to be able to survive the sea without help, even if they were able to beat the water pressure and find their way out from under the ice. There were no cabins here. No fires to warm themselves against. And there was no way Shaw would make it.

An idea occurred to Maddock. "What about the torpedo tubes? Can we get out that way?"

"Too narrow," Bones said. "Even if we were buck naked we'd never get through. Not even a skinny runt like Professor. Besides, if I'm going to get naked it's not going to be with a bunch of dudes."

They were well and truly trapped in this tin can.

Footsteps along the corridor heralded the return of Professor and Willis. If they were going to die down there then they would die together.

"I could go back in there, see if I can loose another charge—assuming it costs another five minutes, it might make a difference. I ain't sure how much of one though, but anything is better than nothing, right? We might be able to blow the hatch." Willis suggested.

"How long have we got left?" Maddock asked.

"Eight minutes," Willis replied. "Less when I get in there."

"If we lose another five minutes when you do..." Maddock didn't need to spell it out. Three minutes to get out of there, cover the distance to the hatch and blow it before the charges in the engine room went off. "Professor?"

"Willis is faster than me."

Maddock considered the idea. It wasn't enough time. Or was it? "Do it."

Willis set off running. He was back soon, charging along the corridor with Bones and Professor right behind him. Maddock tried to help the injured Shaw back to his feet, but the man was done. He couldn't even begin to help himself.

"I said leave me," Shaw rasped. "It's over, Maddock. Even if he manages to blow the hatch there's no way that you'll be able to get me there and out of this thing before it gets pulled under."

"Of course we will."

The man shook his head. "I'm not a child. I know what's happening here. Let me go."

Maddock knew that Shaw was right, but he couldn't just leave him behind.

"Let me help you," Shaw said. "Prop me up against the door. I'll keep it closed, so even if the engine room fills quickly I'll buy you a few more seconds. That extra minute or two might make all the difference. Let me die trying to save you. OK? Let me do that."

Maddock wanted to argue. The blast from the hatch shook the sub, earning deep groans from the hull as it shivered against the ice.

"Cheer up, it might never happen." Shaw managed a wry smile.

They were both going to die down here. Another howl of metal tearing came from deep within the submarine. The entire structure groaned around him.

"Go!" Shaw pressed himself up against the door.

A second blast thundered.

Maddock didn't move. He knelt down beside Shaw. The solider had his eyes closed. He reached into his thick jacket and snapped off his dog tags. "I'll make sure these get home. I promise."

Shaw didn't say anything.

He didn't need to.

There were no words.

Maddock pushed himself to his feet and ran for the middle of the sub and the hatch that would take him up to the surface. The *Echo II* shook and groaned with every step, the incline increasing second by second as she started to tear free of her icy prison. He didn't look back. He didn't want to see Nate Shaw slumped against that door. Maybe he'd be able to hold the relentless rush of the tide back for a few seconds, no more than that, surely? But Maddock couldn't let him die down in the cold and dark in vain. He'd use those seconds because they'd come at such a staggeringly high price.

The dim light flickered on and off around him, plunging the corridor into darkness and the submarine slipped another inch, then there was a sudden lurch as she dropped a foot. Maddock lost his footing, thrown forward. He hit the deck hard, and reached out for support, on his feet again only to stumble and sprawl over one of the dead Russian submariners as the lights flickered back into life.

"It's no good," Bones shouted to him as he closed the last few feet. "It won't budge."

So that was it.

It had all been in vain.

Willis and Professor dropped back down, finding a place to plant their feet without treading on corpses. They both looked dejected, completely without hope. There had to be something they hadn't tried. Something that could still get them out of there. They only had seconds before the submarine slipped down into the water where no one would bother trying to salvage it.

The *Echo II* shifted again, slipping another foot deeper as metal scraped on ice, filling the inside of the boat with a chorus of haunting groans.

Maddock almost missed the clanging of something moving on the outside of the hull.

"Quiet." He lifted a hand to silence the others. "Did you hear that?"

"What is it?" Bones asked.

"We going under?" Willis looked down at his own feet

as if expecting to see water and ice rising up.

An instant later they were flooded by a pool of light as the hatch opened above them.

TWENTY THREE

"Hello boys," the voice called from above. "You might want to get a move on, I don't think this is going to hold much longer."

"Zara, you're a sight for sore eyes." Maddock felt a surge of emotion that was part joy, part relief, and part vindication, so glad she'd proved him right. The boat moved again, slipping deeper. It wouldn't hold for long. The others started up the ladder as water started rushing in through the bulkhead. It came fast, rushing in with a torrent of churning whitecaps as it swelled to fill every inch of the depressurized hull. It pulled at his legs as he climbed, the last man up the ladder. He felt the wash of ice cold water against his legs. He gave a final glance back down into the darkness. Nate Shaw was gone. Those few seconds had made a difference. He would do everything he could to make sure the man's family knew that. It wasn't much, but it was all that he could do. He didn't want them receiving a form letter saying he died a hero and nothing else. He would sit with them face-to-face and explain how Nate had saved his life. He owed the man that.

The submarine lurched again.

Someone shouted from above him.

If he didn't get off the conning tower he'd be dragged under with the dead man and no amount of good intentions would make a damned bit of difference.

The submarine gave out another groan.

Maddock climbed faster, hand over hand, rising toward the light.

Water rushed in below him, washing over the bodies of the dead Russians as it surged up the stairwell.

Hands reached down for Maddock as voices cried out for him to hurry.

He scrambled up the last couple of steps and stumbled as he reached the razor-wire shards of ice frosted onto the metal. Bones grabbed his hood and hauled him to his feet as he struggled to get any purchase on the floor beneath him.

The others were already on the ice and running toward the safety of the shore.

Behind them another six feet of the *Echo II* slipped beneath the ice.

"Move!" Bones urged. Maddock saw in an instant why. It had been a double-trap; not only had the submarine been trapped in the ice, the ice had been trapped in place by the bulk of the submarine. Without it, the integrity of the ice sheet had begun to fail. Massive fissures spread across the surface, black lines promising a bleak death if they were caught out in the middle of the sheet once it broke free. The air was filled with the cracks of the ice slowly tearing itself apart. It wouldn't hold for long. It couldn't.

He looked at Bones. The big man nodded.

"Butch and Sundance?" Bones asked.

"Didn't they both die?" Maddock wasn't sure it was the best example.

Bones grabbed his hand and together the pair of them took a running jump from the conning tower, arms and legs flailing as they kicked out for the solid ice that looked and, impossibly long way down.

They landed hard, the ice beneath them shrieking as their weight drove it down, and started to slide remorselessly toward the water. Maddock scrambled to his feet, Bones beside him, grinning, and they ran for their lives as the sub went down.

Arms and legs pumping furiously, chin down, ice cold air burning his lungs, he struggled for breath, every sinew on fire as he ran on a surface that shifted constantly beneath him. He didn't look back, didn't look down, he focused on the safety of the distant land mass.

With a shriek that rent his soul, a great sheet of ice sheared away beneath his feet.

Maddock lost his balance as it tipped and shifted, but caught it again before he was bucked, but that didn't stop a gulf opening up between him and the main ice sheet still anchored to the shore. There was no way he could jump it, not weighed down by the Arctic gear he wore. He didn't have time to think or weigh up his options; he had to act on instinct as the ground he stood on started to drift away from the shore. Somehow, Bones was on the other side of the gulf. He'd only been a step or two ahead of Maddock when the ice had torn apart, now he was getting further away all the time.

The others were calling to him, urging him to jump but their voices were just a cacophony of noise. He steadied himself for a moment, making sure that he had his balance. He would have one chance to get this right.

If he got it wrong he may as well have stayed on the submarine.

He took a step back, and another and another until the ice started to tilt backward, his weight on the wrong side of its pivot-point. He started to run, the sudden shift of his weight pushing the ice back down as his boots skidded on it. He threw his arms forward, jumping, legs kicking out in a desperate attempt to get a few more inches out of the leap. His boots came down hard on the ice, and it began to break away beneath the impact of his landing. He kept running until someone grabbed hold of him, pulling him onto a safer surface.

Dane slumped to the ground, breathing hard.

He couldn't quite believe they'd gotten out of there alive.

"That was interesting," he said, as the submarine tilted almost upright, the weight of the water inside dragging it down. No one would come to recover the bodies of the dead; that metal coffin would serve them for eternity.

"Did they get the egg?" Leopov asked.

Maddock answered with a question of his own: "You want to tell me why you deserted the camp?"

"You know why."

"Humor me," Maddock said.

"My orders are to stay close to you. I overheard you planning to light out. I was ready to go as soon as you left. Besides, there was something you needed to know."

"And what's that?"

"The Russian. He wasn't making sense even when he was talking, but he said something that I thought you should hear. He claimed to be a descendant of Rasputin."

"The Mad Monk?" said Professor.

"Whether he is or he isn't doesn't really make any difference," she said. "He kept talking about one of the lost Fabergé eggs. He said that his ancestor had designed it to take revenge on the people who were betraying him. There was something inside it that would bring about the fall of the people who had betrayed his country. I wasn't sure if he meant the people who betrayed Russia back in the days before the revolution, or now."

"Now?"

"Now meaning President Gorbachev," she said.

"Gorbachev?" Maddock cocked his head. "He's on the brink of ending the Cold War. How's that a betrayal?"

"Not everyone wants it to end," Professor observed. "There are plenty of people who want things to remain the way they've always been. That revolution was hard fought and bloody. Any kind of change now is weakness in their eyes. A betrayal of the sacrifice of their people."

"And our mad Russian thinks he can use the egg to bring down Gorbachev?" Maddock shook his head. He couldn't quite add up these two and twos without making five. How could a man out here, cut off from society, think he could change the world by bringing down one of the two most powerful men in it?"

"I think he's planning on assassinating him," she said. "Using the egg somehow to fulfill Rasputin's destiny."

"Give him a gift with the means of his death inside it? Do you think that something that was made a century ago could still work?"

"Maybe," said Professor.

"Maybe he intends to put something else inside it? Ricin maybe? Sarin?" Leopov said. "We have intelligence that suggests biological weapons are being tested in secret here on this island."

"*Now* you tell us," said Bones.

"I know I can't be the only one thinking it, so I'll say it: what's it got to do with us?" asked Willis. "We're talking about Russians killing Russians. I ain't gonna cry over it, put it that way. Let them kill each other if that's what they want. Better that than kill the rest of the world."

"Think about it. They blame the West, and what happens?" Professor said. "This won't just get rid of a leadership they are unhappy with, it'll set peace back decades and unite Russia behind whoever promises revenge on America."

"Meaning whoever promises to push that big red button," said Bones.

"Meaning *we* have got to stop them," Maddock reasoned. "Because no one else knows there's even a threat."

"Exactly," Professor agreed. "At worst, we stop a few more people getting killed. At best we stop another World War."

"And at the very least it will make sure that Lewis and Shaw didn't die for nothing," Bones finished.

Willis couldn't argue with that. He nodded.

"We'll never catch up with them," Leopov pointed out. "They're long gone."

"So we work out where they'll be heading and go

there. Best guess?"

"There's the old Gulag. That's where they seem to have been conducting experiments."

"I've seen it on the map," said Professor. "There's no way we can get there before them. They're on Skidoos, we're on foot."

"There's nothing to say that we have to get there *before* them," said Maddock. "After all, we have one advantage over them."

"And what's that?" asked Bones.

"They think we're dead."

TWENTY FOUR

Maddock was impressed by the way that Leopov managed to keep up with them this time. She pushed herself hard, determined not to be the one who let the team down. She'd made her own way across the mountains despite the risk the sabertooths presented. He liked to think he was a decent judge of people and he suspected something more than anger over being left behind was driving her on. He didn't know what, but now more than ever he was absolutely sure it was about more than following orders. Maybe she'd been promised something if this all worked out the way top brass wanted? Stranger things had happened.

"You do realize that just because we're dead doesn't mean that we'll be able to take out a group of Spetsnaz without dying all over again." Willis was trying to keep things light, but wasn't helping.

"How far?" Maddock asked, ignoring the comment.

"A couple of klicks," Professor said. "We should be able to see it when we get over the next ridge. I'll go on ahead and take a look." The skidoo tracks turned off to the right to avoid the difficulty of the incline, but going as the crow flies had to save some time. Maddock trusted the other man to get them where they needed to be.

"We'll be right behind you," Maddock said.

The top of the ridge gave them a clear view of the Gulag. That meant that anyone in the watchtowers had a clear view of them cresting the rise, too. It was a grim place. A concrete block prison behind high wire fence. There were few windows, and those he saw were so small they could barely let any light through. He signaled to the others to drop, presenting as small a target as possible. The white of their Arctic coats would act as camouflage, but not if they were standing upright on top of the ridge like sitting ducks. Beyond the wire fence, a helicopter waited. That explained how they were planning on getting out of there.

Maddock took a moment to look through the binoculars. Even in the dull light visibility was good. "No one's moving around."

"Are you sure? I thought I saw a reflection from up in the watchtower." Bones raised a hand to point toward a dark shape up there. Maddock trained the glasses on it. He saw the figure, leaning against the rail, unmoving.

"Something's not right," he said, tracking across the open area behind the barbed wire fence. In the shadows, close to the nearest building there were other shapes. Shapes that, when he focused on them, looked a lot like bodies lying on the ground.

"We need to get closer," said Bones.

"Not all of us. I don't want us taking more chances than we absolutely have to."

"We're all in this together, Maddock."

"I know we are, but the more of us that go down there, the more likely that we'll get spotted." The skidoos were just coming around the ridge, traveling in single file toward the main building. They stopped some distance from it and dismounted. Maddock didn't dare move, even the slightest sound or flicker of movement could betray them. They waited until the last of the Russians had headed inside before they made their move. "Check out the skidoos," Maddock said. "See if there's anything we can use. We're not going to have long before they move out. We need to make sure the chopper's out of commission, that should buy us a bit longer."

He was the first to his feet. Leopov was a heartbeat behind him. It was hard for him to tell her to stay with one of the others, she'd earned the right to stand beside him when she'd saved their lives. That, and if past experience was anything to go on, she'd happily ignore anything he said. She was determined to stick to him like a second shadow so he might as well just accept it.

He didn't look back, just made his way down the ridge to the fence.

The figure in the watchtower didn't move, even though he must have been able to see them as they moved closer. Maddock was pretty sure that the man was not sleeping. Why was there a dead man in the watchtower?

The shadows lengthened as the sun sank quickly below the horizon.

The area close to the building was almost black, so thick was the shadow already.

As he reached the fence Maddock saw at least another half a dozen bodies lying on the ground between the watchtower and the helicopter.

He signaled the others forward, knowing he could be leading his team into a death trap.

TWENTY FIVE

Breaking through the fence was easy enough; Bones carried a pair of cutters in his bag that were strong enough to slice through the heavy gauge wire. Within a couple of minutes he'd cut a line up through the chain links wide enough for them to crawl through.

Maddock led the way with Bones and Leopov close behind, Willis and Professor brought up the rear.

He stayed close to the fence, conscious of a need for an exfiltration route should things go haywire before they were even halfway across the yard. He kept the corpses between him and the open ground. There was nothing to show how the men had died, or any clue as to how long ago it had happened. There was no stench of decay in the sub-zero temperature.

"What do you think killed them?" Maddock whispered, thinking aloud.

He didn't expect an answer, but Leopov gave him one he really hadn't considered. It sent a shiver bone deep.

"Honestly? I think the prisoners held here were used as guinea pigs for the weapons they were testing."

It made sense. Someone had decided his team didn't need to know what they were walking into. He'd make that hurt them in the long run. He signaled for her to follow, then took off running, covering the killing ground between where they were and the first of the buildings fast.

He hit the wall just as a door opened and someone emerged from the main building. If the figure looked to his left they would be caught.

He didn't. He walked straight across the yard toward the helicopter.

Maddock pulled Leopov deeper into the shadows,

pressing them both against the wall. Bones didn't need anyone to tell him what he needed to do; Maddock could feel his warm breath behind him. Professor crept along to the corner, then disappeared around it out of sight. He didn't know where Willis was.

The man didn't so much as look at the dead bodies as he passed them.

"We're going to have to stop him," Maddock whispered. "If he gets into that thing there's no way on earth we are going to be able to keep him here."

As if on cue Willis appeared on the other side of the fence with a length of chain dangling from his right hand.

Maddock looked at it, then back at the helicopter, grasping what Willis had in mind. "We've found a stash of gasoline too, so Professor's taking a look to see what he can rig up. There's some old glass bottles in a storage shed along with a bag of old rags from the prison, so at worst we're going in hot with Molotov cocktails."

Maddock drew the chain through the fence.

It was a long shot and they'd be exposing themselves, but he had to do something.

"Stay here," he said to Leopov.

She nodded in agreement. For once he was pretty sure she was going to do as she'd been told.

Maddock waited for the man to climb into the helicopter. Once he was in his seat he was facing away from them, meaning he could make his move. Bones helped carry the chain so it wasn't dragging on the ground. The moved in a tight crouch, fast.

The engine burst into life, the rotor blades turning slowly before they'd covered half the distance. The blades gradually picked up speed, whipping up dust and debris as they did. Maddock glanced at the open doorway. There was only darkness inside. There was no way of knowing how long they had before the rest of the Spetsnaz team came to join the party.

Twenty yards from the helicopter, the pilot made their approach.

A couple of seconds later and they might have been able to get into it, and him out of it, before he realized what had hit him. Then they'd have had control of the bird. Too late for that. The pilot took her up, the runners lifting a few inches from the ground as it started to turn. The tail swung away from them.

He realized what the pilot had in mind; he wasn't trying to flee, he was using the machine as a weapon.

The chopper continued to rise slowly, ten feet, twelve, fifteen and then a started to dip toward them as the tail rose in the air. Maddock and Bones took a step backward, battered by the downdraft.

The helicopter moved toward them, the blades spinning into a blur now, offering the promise of death.

They could press themselves up against the chain link fence, which would offer them some protection from the pilot—but it would also make them sitting ducks for the rest of his team. Or they could be gladiators, taking on the great beast with nothing but a chain.

"Throw it" Maddock shouted above the roar of the blades, pointing up toward the rotor cuff and willing Bones to read his mind.

In a single fluid motion they hurled the heavy chain into the air. Every muscle and sinew strained as Maddock sent the chain arcing upward.

They had one chance.

The steel links clattered against the blades as they spun, metal grinding against metal as it caught in the rotor and was dragged inward. The ends of the chain spun wildly, clattering against the glass windshield in front of the pilot's face, creating deep cracks that widened in seconds to fissures. One end of the chain was whipped up and hit the blade again before being wound so tightly around the mechanism the engine shrieked under the extra strain, the helicopter bucking and twisting as the pilot wrestled with the stick trying to keep some sort of control and get it up out of there. The bird began to rise, but it was rocking violently, no real balance to the ascent as the blades slowed.

The engine screamed with the effort, but it wasn't staying airborne. The tail swung wildly, turning and clipping the top of the fence. The tail rotor sliced into the chain links as the machine twisted in the air. The tip of the main blade touched the ground, metal digging deep into the ice, twisting, bending and buckling as it did, gouging into the ground. Chips of ice and metal flew all around, hard as bullets and every bit as deadly as the blades tore apart, sheering the bolts holding them.

Maddock ran, never looking away from the out of control machine as the cabin hit the ice. Too late, he realized that it was heading to the wall where he'd left Leopov. The helicopter hit the wall before he could even shout her name.

He watched as the pilot desperately tried to get out. The doorframe had buckled. He pushed and kicked at it, but it wasn't opening. There was a moment of peace as the engine fell silent. That was the worst of it, that second of silence and seeing his face up against the glass, before the helicopter burst into flames. There was no chance of him making out alive. The heat was sudden and intense, the shockwave from the blast hurling Maddock off his feet.

He hit the deck hard, skidding as he scrambled back to his feet. He couldn't see Leopov anywhere.

"Zara!" he yelled, his voice drowned by the crackling flames. He had no way of knowing if she could hear him.

No reply.

He pushed himself back toward the blazing wreckage, the staggering heat driving him back three steps for every two forward.

Bones yelled. He couldn't hear any of the words for

the roaring inferno, but sound was enough to turn his head so he saw the Russian gunman come charging out of the building. In a heartbeat the rifle in his hands was aimed squarely at Maddock's chest.

He raised his hands in surrender. He was trying to buy time for Bones or one of the other guys to do something. Judging by the bodies on the ground the Russians weren't taking prisoners.

Maddock was helpless. There was nothing he could do. He heard the shot and waited to for the pain.

Nothing.

How had the guy missed from point blank range? There was no second shot. The Russian crumpled, a blood red rose opening in the center of his chest.

He followed the direction of the shot back up to the watchtower.

Leopov stood there, leaning against the barrier with the dead sentry's rifle in her hand.

TWENTY SIX

They came out with guns blazing.

Leopov picked off the first man before he knew where the threat was coming from. She was brutally efficient, one shot to the center of mass, another to the head. There was no getting up from that. Then she laid down covering fire for Maddock as he raced to join Bones back at the corner of the building.

Something shifted inside the helicopter, the struts holding the seats into the frame gave way. It was noise, not threat. He ignored it.

"She's good, man, you have to admit it." Bones cast an admiring glance in the woman's direction.

"She's a lifesaver. Now it's all about how long she can hold them back."

Maddock risked a glance around the corner. There was no sign of any of the Russians. They'd taken cover back inside the building. He heard the occasional shot. Nothing sustained. They were taking pot shots up at the woman in the tower.

"That it is, bro. That it is. We've got to do something before they get lucky," Bones said.

It was only a matter of time before one of the stray shots clipped her.

The door swung outward. It was a dozen strides from them. As long as the Russians didn't rush out to storm the tower he'd have long enough to reach it. What he did after that he wasn't so sure about, but he could at least slam it closed and rob them of their line-of-sight on Leopov.

He acted fast, before doubt could creep in.

He snatched up a piece of metal that was still hot from where it had torn free of the wreckage. It would be no defense against a semi-automatic.

He hugged close to the wall, brushing against the concrete blocks until he was close enough to reach out and touch the door. Another shot. He couldn't tell if it came from the tower or from the building.

He was banking on Leopov reading his mind. She fired a single shot into the open doorway.

Maddock seized the chance. He hit the door hard, and slammed it into place, trying to force the sliver of metal underneath the frame to wedge it closed.

A staccato burst of gunfire erupted from inside and tore through the door, showering him with splinters of wood.

He pulled back against the wall, grateful for the thickness of concrete between him and the Russian bullets. The door was shredded. If he'd been behind it he would have been cut in half. He needed to get Leopov out of the tower. His pistol was one thing, but the gun she'd taken from the dead sentry was another altogether. They needed to match the Russians shell for shell.

Bones had read his thoughts.

The Cherokee reacted to Maddock's move, charging toward the sentry tower. He could see Leopov making her way down the ladder, exposed.

"Wanna start a fire then, boss?" Willis said, appearing at the other side of the fence again.

"Let's light this place up like the Bicentennial," Maddock said.

Willis chuckled. "You're a man out of time; that's so Seventies. You couldn't just go with the Fourth of July?"

Maddock rolled his eyes.

The overwhelming smell of gasoline filled the air. Willis carried a box stuffed with a dozen or so glass bottles, all of various shapes and sizes, each with a rag wedged into its neck.

"That's me," Maddock said, distracted by the sight of Bones and Leopov racing back across the killing ground toward them. "Time for the fireworks."

"What's the plan?" Willis asked.

"We take out the bad guys, get the egg back, save the girl and get the hell out of Dodge. You know, that kind of thing. Nothing to it."

"Not that this girl looks like she needs saving."

"No. But maybe I was calling you the girl?" Maddock grinned.

"Funny."

"I like to think so."

Bones reached the wall. "Ready to smoke those bad boys out?"

"I think we give them a couple of minutes then we open the door," Maddock said.

A look passed between the four of them. Bones broke the strained silence. "Either I'm missing the joke or you've lost your mind." He had a tight hold on the gun. Leopov had a huge smile on her face. Maddock almost told her she'd done a good job, but if she wanted to be treated like one of them she was going to have to get used to being taken for granted.

"I'm not sure we've got much of a choice. We can't rain down holy hell on them. We need to get in after them, or smoke them out, if we're going to complete the mission. Remember we're here to get the egg. Simple as that. They have it. They're in there. We want it. We need to go in and get it or bring them out and take it off them."

"You make it sound simple," Leopov said.

"Logistically it is."

"What about secondary objectives?" she asked. "If the egg is some sort of assassination tool, how about we rig the place to blow—we wouldn't get the egg back, but the Russians wouldn't have it either."

"We'd still have to go in to make sure it had been destroyed. We couldn't risk someone finding it in the rubble, especially as we don't have any idea of what's inside or or how well its contents are protected," Maddock said.

"He's got a point," Bones said. "So we go in after it."

A single semi-automatic, four handguns and a box of Molotov cocktails didn't seem like much to go up against a crack team of Russian Spetsnaz who were armed to the teeth. The odds were stacked in the Russians' favor. Maddock had never been on to worry about odds when he had a job to do. Maddock was working on the theory that the enemy wouldn't be eager to die; self-preservation should take precedence. The problem was some things were worth dying for. What if the Russians saw this as one of them?

"We could try negotiating with them," Leopov suggested.

"You think they'll just hand it over if we ask nicely?" Maddock asked. "They've got us out gunned, we're on their soil risking a major international incident. And let's be honest, for all we know they could be radioing for reinforcements right now."

"You make a compelling case," she agreed. "Let's go in through the front door then."

TWENTY SEVEN

Willis held one of the bottles at the ready.

He'd found a length of wood and used the still-burning wreckage of the helicopter to turn it into a blazing torch. Admittedly, the conflagration was overkill, but it worked. They made their way back to the doors on the other side of the building where Professor was keeping an eye on the skidoos. He welcomed the thought of the Russkies charging out. He was ready to do some serious damage to East-West relations.

Maddock kept the others back as he moved past the skidoos.

Bones had handed over the heavy artillery. Even so he'd be at Maddock's side, ready to take down all comers.

Willis hefted the burning cocktail, ready to hurl it through the doorway.

Leopov's idea of trying to talk their way out of this without bloodshed appealed, but why on earth would a bunch of fanatics seemingly involved in a plot to assassinate their own president simply hand over Pandora's Egg? It was naïve in the extreme.

Maddock eased the door open.

No gunshots greeted the slow groan. He waited, holding the team back.

Nothing.

The Russians waited somewhere in the near darkness within. Ready.

Maddock gestured for the team to move in. They took a couple of steps over the threshold and waited for the volley of gunfire. Nothing.

No. Not nothing.

In the silence Maddock heard a dry click and knew they were screwed. The point man had tripped some kind of trap.

"Get out!" he yelled, snatching hold of Leopov's arm and pushing her back toward the open door. She stumbled as the first bullet dug into the concrete where her head had been a heartbeat before. They bundled back through the still open doorway out into the open air. Bones was on point. He had no idea if the man had been cut down until he saw him stumble out of the door behind them a few seconds later, bleeding. He'd taken a hit up in the soft flesh of his left bicep. His Arctic jacket was stained with blood. The big man didn't so much as wince as he came out of there.

Maddock dragged Leopov to one side as a hail of bullets filled the air with deafening noise. It was pointless firing back into the darkness.

Willis didn't hesitate. He flung the first of his blazing bombs inside.

The glass bottle hit the concrete floor and exploded with a gout of flame which seemed to suck in the air from outside to swell its angry fire before it died back. Amongst the roar of the flames Maddock heard a scream. At least one of the Russians was hurt. Willis launched a second bottle. The burning rag blazed a trail through the air as it turned end over end before spinning away into the line of flames beyond the threshold.

The scream was louder this time. A direct hit. A burning man staggered out through the doorway, dropping to his knees as the fire tore up his body, fusing cloth and flesh into one blackened, charred, mess of sores. The flames licked at his face. He brought his Kalashnikov up, spewing bullets until the trigger dry-clicked on the empty cartridge. The burning man didn't release his grip. He couldn't. It wasn't a good way to die. He fell forward, dead, still burning, the cocktail soaking into his skin. The air reeked with the stench of charred meat.

Maddock saw others moving in the shadows behind

him.

Bones ran toward the fallen man, trying to pull the coat off him but it was too late. And, truthfully, it was for the best.

"Leave him," a voice from the doorway called. It was the leader of the Spetsnaz team. He had his submachine gun in front of him, ready to cut down Bones if the big man turned on him. He seemed fascinated by his enemy's concern for his fallen comrade, as if it was an alien concept. "This is not my fight and it wasn't his either. The man you want is inside. He is insane, believe me, there is no reasoning with him."

"What do you propose?" Maddock called across the distance, not willing to believe it could be this easy.

"I would rather take my chances with Mother Russia than be part of his madness. But if you go in there, know that you enter at your peril." The man had a curiously formal, old-fashioned way of talking.

"What about the rest of your men?"

"The rest? That was the only one left to take home." He looked down at the body beside Bones. Maddock weighed up their options. There was a chance that the Russian was stalling them, that he'd sent word for more men to finish what he had started, but he sounded like a man who was broken, all of the fight beaten out of him.

It was impossible to believe that a couple of bottles of gasoline achieved that.

The man emerged from the darkness, crouched to put his weapon on the ground, then walked slowly toward Professor and the skidoos.

"Where's the egg?" Maddock asked.

The Russian grimaced. "He has it in there."

Their new captive held up his arms while Bones frisked him.

"He's clean. What do you want to do with him, chief?"

"What are you going to do if I let you walk out of

here?" Maddock asked.

"Go." The look in his eyes told Maddock it was an honest answer.

"Okay. Get the hell out of here. Don't turn around or I'll put a bullet in your skull. Do we understand each other?"

The Russian nodded. "May God go with you," he said, looking back toward the black hole that was the open door, and whatever lay across that blazing threshold. He crossed himself, then clambered onto one of the skidoos. Professor stepped back to let the man twist the ignition and power away from the camp, churning snow in his wake.

They watched as the skidoo receded in the distance.

None of them spoke.

Bones bent down to retrieve the fallen man's weapon. "That was weird," he said, breaking the silence. "Something happened in there. It doesn't smell right."

"Which is why we're going in," Maddock agreed. He turned to Leopov. "I'm not asking this time, Leopov. I don't want you getting hurt when we go in there. Stay back with Professor. We'll call you when the building's secure. Ok?" She nodded. No argument.

Maddock and Bones headed back inside the building, no idea what was waiting for them inside.

On the threshold, Maddock stopped and turned to Professor. "Was our gear still on the skidoos?" Professor nodded. "Fire up the radio, get word back to the ship. We're not hanging around here." With that, he motioned for Bones to go in with him. They stepped into the smoky darkness as the cocktail's fire burned out.

TWENTY EIGHT

They came across a few bodies as they made their way inside but these were not soldiers; they were thin to the point of emaciation, skin stretched tight across cheek bones and shoulders. They were brittle and broken.

"Prisoners," Bones said.

Maddock wasn't so sure. "That, or victims of the same thing that's inside that egg."

"Guinea pigs?"

Maddock nodded. "And if I'm right, there's no way of knowing if we've been contaminated simply by coming in here, or if it's got some kind of half-life and is already burned out."

"Pleasant thought, dude. Maybe Professor's got a theory; he's usually got an answer for everything."

"Personally, I'd rather not know. We're going to have to do this regardless."

From somewhere further along the corridor came a deep bass thrum that resonated through the walls all around them. It could have been a generator firing into life, or a drill. A huge drill. Sound echoed through the concrete, becoming increasingly distorted as it did so."

"This way," Maddock said, taking them toward the noise. They turned right to face concrete walls splattered red. The first thing they saw was the smear of blood along the floor like a trail of breadcrumbs for them to follow. Maddock cursed under his breath but took one cautious step after another until they reached a body which had been dragged along the ground.

"Spetsnaz." Maddock recognized the emblem tattooed onto the man's neck. He checked for a pulse. Nothing. As he turned the corpse over he saw that the Russian's chest had been torn open to expose splintered ribs. Internal organs shifted and started to spill as he lowered him back down again.

The noise came again.

This time Maddock knew that the sound had come from whatever had done this to the dead Russian. It wasn't a drill or a generator. It was the deep-throated growl of the monsters they'd faced out on the ice.

He gave the nod for Bones to move on. As they took the next corner it became abundantly clear why the Spetsnaz leader had been so eager to leave.

Three more of his men had been torn apart, limbs severed from their bodies, chewed and torn, ripped and covered in so much blood there could have been forty instead of four dead men in the room. The fourth lay in the doorway, wedging the door open. His head had been crushed by vice-like jaws.

They looked at each other, at the corpses, and then back at each other. The place was quiet now. Too quiet. The door ahead led to wherever the creatures had made their lair. They had a choice. Move the body and allow the door to close—and hopefully trap the animal in there—or go inside and face the thing.

The problem was the egg. They had no way of knowing where it was, but the crappiest laws of the universe guaranteed the creatures were between them and it. That was just the way the world worked.

"I'm going in. You secure the rest of the building after the door closes behind me."

There was no argument from Bones, despite the fact that separating didn't feel like the smartest move. He gave the briefest of nods and dragged the dead man out of the way. A sticky trail of blood smeared along the floor. Maddock tried not to step in it, but it was impossible. The man had spilled his guts across the floor and the staircase on the other side. There was nowhere that wasn't stained dark with the stuff.

Maddock went through the door.

He stopped and listened on the other side after the door closed behind him.

The path ahead was lit by dull lights.

He had to tread carefully, and softly.

As he listened, he realized that there were two distinct sounds, one animalistic, the great cat's growl, the other the voice of a man, speaking soft and low in Russian. Neither man nor beast was aware of his presence.

Maddock held his gun at the ready, descending into the darker levels of the basement. The stone steps had been hewn into the rock. At the bottom, he paused again to listen. The sounds traveled eerily around the rock, carrying a strange echo that made him realize that this was more than a simple cellar dug into the ground. The walls and the ceiling above him were, in the main, roughly hewn. Myriad cables ran along them, connecting machine after machine. Numbers flashed on screens that meant nothing to Maddock. Some of them could just as easily be some fancy washing machine as they could be the control center for a guided missile system. It wasn't his job to work out what they were. He just had to get the egg and get out of there with the rest of his team. Or at least the ones who were left.

He wasn't going to be able to count on surprise. He needed to think this through. The animal would have his scent.

He reached the end of the passage, and as he turned to enter what seemed to be a cavernous laboratory hewn out of the ground, he saw the wild-eyed Russian crouching beside one of the sabertooth tigers. His first thought was that the beast was one they'd faced down in the mountains. No, it was smaller, caged in this space. How many more of this extinct species could there possibly be?

The beast opened its mouth and roared, but it didn't move an inch closer to him.

The Russian rose to his feet and stood beside it, one hand resting on its great head. The creature showed no sign of objecting to his proximity. Was it tame?

"Ah," said the Russian in heavily accented English. "Join us, please."

"You can speak English?" Maddock shouldn't have been surprised, but realized that meant the man had understood everything they'd said in his presence despite the fact he had only babbled in Russian. He'd played them.

"I can do many things," the man said. "Most importantly for you, I can allow you to leave alive, or I can let Lena here play with you, if you'd prefer. Your choice."

Maddock shook his head; it was an involuntary movement. Close up, the beast was every bit as threatening as the ones that had attacked them in the mountains, despite its smaller stature. Its menace seemed almost amplified because it was more restrained, controlled, making it all the more obvious it was the madman's weapon.

Maddock took a breath. The Sabertooth matched it with a rumble, jowls curling back into a snarl. The creature was tensed, ready to spring at the word of its master.

Maddock said, "All I want is the egg. I'm not after you, I don't care about this place, or your pet. My mission was to bring Pandora's Egg home. I can't leave here without it."

"This." The Russian reached into the depths of his pocket to fish out the exquisitely crafted Fabergé egg. "Do you even know what it is?"

"I don't need to know. I just need to do what I'm told."

"Ah, the military mantra. Let me educate you. What you call Pandora's Egg, was made by the great Fabergé. Every year he would fashion an Easter egg to be presented as a gift to the Russian royal family. Many of them have survived, but not all. Some were lost during the chaos of the revolution. This one was designed by my ancestor

Grigori Rasputin. It contains something as powerful as anything ever created in this place. Inside its brittle shell is Romanov's Bane, revenge on the kind of people who betray the spirit of Mother Russia." He ran a hand along the tiger's back. The creature turned its head to look at him for a moment before turning its gaze back to Maddock.

Ancestor? Was this man claiming to be descended from the Mad Monk who had become so entangled in the court of the Tzars and their downfall? Could he have created some kind of nerve agent or biological weapon could have survived this long hidden inside the egg? Was that what had killed the people in this place? The men on the submarine? Was the Russian immune to it? A shudder passed through him as he realized the much more likely alternative that the man was willing to die for his revenge.

"How did you manage to steal it?" Maddock asked, moving a step closer, keeping his hands visible, knowing it would make him seem less threatening, even with the gun in his hand. "You did steal it, didn't you?"

"One cannot steal what is rightfully his." The Russian's voice remained calm, even.

"Right, and I suppose you've never heard the story about the evil released from Pandora's Box never being able to be put back inside again?"

The tiger strained forward, opening its mouth on those vicious teeth that gave it its name and releasing a roar of defiance. The Russian's touch was enough to hold it at bay.

For now.

But there was no way he could get close enough to the Russian to take the egg without the big cat going for him.

"You are a sanctimonious, condescending young man who knows very little about the world. That is not your fault. You are a military man. As you say, you do not need to know these things. This will stop the enemies of our great country, those who would make peace with the West.

Those of our own people who would allow the capitalists to corrupt our nation."

"What about the innocents? Don't they factor into this?"

"Innocents? There are no innocents in this world. When this gift is opened there will be no innocents there. It will be presented to a weak Russian and a corrupt American. There will be the yes men and advisers who hang onto their every word, and the media who get pleasure out of the weakening of our state. But no innocents." His voice rose with each line. There was an anger and a passion in the words as he spat them.

His control over the tiger relaxed as he lifted his hand from its back.

The cat understood that he'd been given freedom to act.

It sprang forward, full body rising, claws out, too fast for Maddock to react, closing the ten feet between them in a heartbeat. He couldn't do anything. The weight of the beast hit him square in the chest, hammering the air from his lung. His arm went back, the gun spinning out of his grasp. The sabertooth's momentum drove him to the floor, the beast's weight slamming him down. He could taste the cat's meaty breath in the air. He could feel the heat of it on his face.

Claws pierced his coat.

They snagged against his flesh, tearing.

The big cat lifted its head back one last time, unleashing a final roar of victory before snapping his jaws.

Maddock had no time to fight back, and no leverage or strength to fight with. He felt it all leak out of him with the trickle of blood from the exposed chest wound. The creature tore into him. There was nothing he could do to stop it.

In a heartbeat it could rip into him and tear him apart.

All it would take was one mighty snap of its jaws to

cleave his head from his shoulders.

Maddock reached out desperately, stretching his fingertips, trying to snag hold of his gun. He knew that it was already too late. Even if he could catch hold of it there was no way he'd be able to fire a bullet to stop the arrival of bloody death.

He was a dead man.

A crack echoed; a sound so out of place, quickly followed by another.

The creature's eyes glazed over, dead, its weight falling onto Maddock's chest and pinning him down as the tiger gave up its grip on life. The sheer weight of the beast was suffocating. He gasped for breath, struggling against the pressure, but saw Bones behind its head.

"You can thank me later," the big man said, stepping over Maddock as he strained to push the dead animal off him.

"Stay back." The Russian held the egg out in front of him. "Stay back or I break this open."

"You break it, you lose your revenge. That isn't going to happen. All these years of festering hate wasted? No."

"Keep back," the Russian repeated.

Maddock gave another heave, succeeding in shifting the weight a little.

He breathed deeply, feeling the pain lift from his chest as he gasped for air. There was something broken in there. A rib or two at least. He just had to hope that it wasn't any worse than that.

"I said keep back," said the Russian.

"Look, we both know that you aren't going to do anything with that thing," Bones said. "So why don't you hand it over?"

"I would rather die."

"That can be arranged." Bones sounded as if he would like nothing better.

Maddock had barely extricated himself from beneath

the dead tiger, kicking his legs free at last, when the Russian flung the egg to the ground.

The delicate ornamental shell cracked open.

Everything seemed to freeze, suspended in a moment that would determine whether they all lived or died.

But, as far as Maddock could tell, nothing happened.

He didn't know what he'd expected; some wisps or curls of noxious gas rising from the two halves, maybe. There was nothing.

The Russian started running, barging past Bones who had clamped his free hand over his mouth.

"Too late!" the Russian cackled. "Romanov's Bane is free! Free!"

Bones grabbed hold of the madman's arm, hauling him back, spinning him and throwing him up against the wall. He slammed a fist into the man's gut, doubling him up. As he sank to his knees, Bones stood over him. When he looked up, all the wild haired fool seemed capable of was more babble, his grip on sanity seemingly lost once more.

"Get out of here," Bones said.

"I'm not leaving you," said Maddock.

"That's good, because I'm not planning on staying here. Just go. Keep your distance. And don't breathe."

"We need an antidote. He has to have it."

"If there is one… if it's here… I'll find it. Just get outside and wait." Maddock was about to argue, but Bones cut him off. "There's no point both of us being exposed any longer than we need to be. Someone has to get off this island. Check the rest of the complex, who knows if there's anything in here."

Maddock knew that his friend was right.

They needed to find the antidote, assuming there was one, but how could they do that without knowing what they were up against? The gas had been colorless and odorless. They'd both been exposed to it. They were both dying. It was as simple as that.

"I'll get him to talk," Bones promised.

Maddock didn't doubt him for a moment.

TWENTY NINE

Maddock took the stairs two at a time, oblivious to the danger. It was all about time now. His chest was stained red with the animal's blood and his own.

"Maddock!" Someone shouted when he emerged into the corridor.

It took him a moment to orient himself. He could see their silhouette backlit in the bright light streaming in through the doorway. "Zara? What the hell are you doing in here? I told everyone to keep out."

"We heard a gunshot. Are you all right? Where's Bones.?"

"I'm fine." He waved her away. "Bones is back there. The egg's been broken—whatever the hell's inside it is out, and we've been exposed, stay back."

"Are you all right?"

"On top of the world. Bones too. But we need to find the antidote, if there is one, to whatever agent or toxin was in there."

"Well this just got a heck of a lot more interesting," Willis said, appearing with Professor behind Leopov's shoulder. "What are we looking for and where are we looking for it?"

"No idea. Anywhere. Everywhere. We don't even know for certain that there is one. If this virus or whatever it is has been inside that egg since the time of Rasputin and the Romanov's there's no guarantee any antidote even survived."

"Are you sure there was anything inside?" Professor asked. "Or if it's still viable?"

"Not a chance I'm prepared to take. There's not going to be anything on board the ship that's going to be able to deal with an unknown virus. The chopper should be on its way to pick us up now, but we're not getting on it if there's even the slightest risk we're going to become Patient Zero and bring a plague to the mainland. Simple as that. So we've got until the chopper gets here to find what we need or we wave it away."

Maddock gave orders for them to work in pairs. It might not cover the whole building as quickly, but it would increase the thoroughness of the search. They just needed to cut out wasted time and not allow themselves to become preoccupied with places where the vaccine was unlikely to be hidden.

Doors led to offices and sleeping quarters that did not look promising. Other doors opened onto bare rooms with only a bench and bars on the windows. There were survivors. They weren't in good shape. Maddock found an old man huddled in a corner, arms wrapped around his knees, knees tucked under his chin, rocking in a ball. He left the cell door open, the man could leave if he wanted to, or stay there and rot.

The next three were the same but the inhabitants had not been so fortunate.

They needed to keep looking. Fast.

Door after door, room after room, cells, offices, they were all the same. Maddock felt like screaming, until finally he opened the doors on a fully equipped laboratory. There was more equipment in the one room than he'd seen in any lab in his life.

"Doesn't it seem weird to you there are two laboratories in this place?" he asked.

"Two?" Leopov said.

"Yeah, there's a full scale lab downstairs, that's where the Russian was." He patted the tear across his Artic jacket where the blood had already begun to crust. "Our little furry friend seemed right at home down there."

"You found one *inside*?"

"Took out the whole Spetsnaz team."

"But inside? That doesn't make sense. Where did it come from? How did it even get inside? Those things don't live in captivity, hell they don't even exist outside of places like this, surely? This island's been inhabited for years. There were expeditions up here long before the Russians laid claim to it."

"I'm not sure it was wild," Maddock said. "More like a guard dog."

"But how would that work?" Leopov frowned. "Aside from the obvious, sabertooth tigers are extinct, so how could anyone have domesticated them? It doesn't make sense."

"Unless they found a way to clone them… is that even possible? I mean that was some lab down there… maybe they've been doing some kind of genetic engineering?"

"I don't know. The only thing any of us know is that something killed those people out in the exercise yard," Leopov said. "I didn't see tooth and claw wounds, so that makes me think it was a virus or nerve agent or something. It's the same thing that took those people out on the submarine, too. Beyond that, it's all just guesswork, and even that's stretching what we know. But if you guys have been exposed, then we're exposed, and we're wasting time we can't afford to."

Maddock knew that she was right.

A noise behind him caused Maddock to turn, gun in hand.

He was a hair's breadth from pulling the trigger when he recognized the man as the prisoner they'd released.

"Has it gone?" he asked, his eyes wild with fear.

"The sabertooth?" Maddock asked.

The man nodded, his head moving rapidly.

Maddock nodded. "It's dead."

The old man walked toward them, pitifully frail.

He reached out to support him, but the man shrugged him away.

And then the strangest thing happened: his face lit up when he saw Leopov.

"Natasha?"

THIRTY

He looked a lot older than the picture she'd been shown back in the briefing. Even so, there was no doubt in her mind that this was Hans Luber. She'd never expected to come face to face with him despite the fact she'd been told that he would be there.

"I'm sorry. You're mistaken." She couldn't think of anything else to say. A shiver raced down the ladder of her spine. She felt her knees tremble and felt momentarily unsteady on her feet.

"Forgive me," he said, a tear forming in the corner of his eye. "You look so like her... my daughter. But you are too young, much too young. I am sorry... we have to get out of here. We have to get out of here before it's too late."

Leopov's brain performed somersaults inside her head. There had always been secrets, things her mother had kept from her, lies she had caught her out on. Could this be another aspect of her lies? She had known so little about the man before the briefing and now, facing him, looking him in the eye and seeing the ghosts there, it was impossible not to think they might be related. He had said that she reminded her of his daughter, Natasha. It was too much of a coincidence to be one, wasn't it?

Natasha.

There were a lot of names in the world, so why pick that one?

"The creature's dead. The crazy guy's gone," Maddock said.

"Crazy?"

"Some kind of descendant of Rasputin."

"Ah, yes, that is Yetsic. He has spent too much time with those creatures of his. It was always a mistake to meddle where nature has moved on… recreating those wretched animals from DNA trapped in the ice for millennia… a mistake… He should have left well enough alone. The man is a fanatic. Dangerous and deranged. And now he has stolen my work and plans to use it to stop the world."

"Your work?" Maddock asked, but the man just shook his head.

Leopov didn't know how much Maddock had been told about Luber. It wasn't her place to fill in any gaps about the old man.

"We need to know about your work, Herr Luber," she said softly. "We need to get you somewhere safe."

There was a light in his eyes as he took his hands away. "You sound so much like her too," he said. "It's uncanny. That lightness in your voice, just like hers. Are you sure that you're not my sweet, sweet girl?"

Leopov took a deep breath, not knowing if she was about to make things better or worse. "Natasha is my mother's name."

He stared at her, seeming to see all the way down inside back through the generations, and nodded, content. "Of course it is. Of course. Is she safe? Tell me she is safe. That is all I ask," he pleaded, his face full of life again as if the years had been stripped away for a moment. "That was the trade. Her life for mine. They said they would kill her if I didn't do what they wanted. How could I risk that? How could I think of myself at a time like that, when they had already killed her mother, when they came knocking on the door for her and made me choose? So many years in this place… so many years alone… tell me she is safe. Please. Tell me…"

The questions were tumbling out so fast that she could barely keep up with them, the only one that didn't was the obvious one from Leopov: *are you my grandfather?* The old man seemed swept up in a tide of nostalgia and fear, taken back to the day the Red Army turned up at his door and demanded he turn himself over to save the woman he loved... She didn't have time to answer even half of the questions before more came.

Somewhere a door slammed.

The old man looked up in panic, gripping her arm tightly.

A voice called out.

"The chopper's coming in. We've got to move now." It was Willis.

"Time's up. We've got to get you off this island" Maddock said.

"He comes with us," Leopov said. It was a statement not a request. "So do you. Leave no man behind."

Maddock shook his head. "We can't risk it. Not when we don't know what we've been exposed to down here."

"So you just stick around here and wait to die? I don't think so, Maddock. This isn't the place to argue. Talk to your Commanding Officer when we're back on the ship and he'll tell you that you've done the right thing."

Maddock shook his head, but he wasn't really arguing, he was trying to make sense of the fact that time had all but run out and they were no further forward. He turned to the old man. He had his own question. "We may have been exposed to whatever it is that Yetsic has got his hands on. Is there some kind of antidote?"

"Yes, yes of course, but if you have been exposed it would need to be administered within the first few minutes. The poor men in the cells next to me died within five minutes when Yetsic carried out his tests. He wanted to be sure it was fast. And painful."

Five minutes.

The Russian had shattered the Fabergé egg closer to ten minutes ago. The countdown had entered its final few moments. Seconds. Maddock tried to think but felt his brain turning muddy as it became increasing difficult to focus on what he wanted to. Sweat trickled down the nape of his neck. He was breathing faster but had no way of knowing if that was down to fear or the contagion.

"The men in the cells around you were tested… why weren't you?"

The man smiled. "I was." He didn't appear to be ill but that didn't have to mean anything. Leopov placed a hand over his in the hope that it might comfort him.

"How long ago?"

"Yesterday."

That didn't make sense. If the others had been so weak they'd died within five minutes there's no way he should have been standing. "How is that possible?"

"Because I tested the antidote on myself once I understood what Yetsic intended. There have been enough deaths in this place… because of me… I wanted to do something… to stop the spread of the contagion… I reverse engineered a solution, a hope for mankind. The virus will mutate. It will do everything it can to survive and spread, and without a vaccine it will become a pandemic. So I gave us hope. Yetsic didn't know. He didn't understand. He has only half a mind for the science. All he cares about is the killing, manifesting his father's legacy… how many of you were exposed?"

"Two. Unless the virus could live on in the bodies in the yard outside?"

Hans Luber shook his head. "No. It doesn't work like that. It doesn't spread from person to person as an airborne pathogen. Not yet anyway, but there's a trigger that could change that. The virus is designed to attach itself onto the common cold without too much difficulty. It is a sophisticated contagion, not a replica of Rasputin's elixir, Romanov's Bane. But that old chemistry serves as the building blocks to the new biological terror. It can be manipulated to attack certain gene sequences, meaning it can be used to target specific genetic identifiers."

"Are you saying it can be made to affect only one particular race?" Leopov asked.

Maddock followed her line of thought, realizing they were talking about a weapon of genocide.

Her question didn't need an answer and it didn't get one.

"Is there more of that vaccine?"

The old man nodded.

"Get it, then get outside. I'm going to get Bones. We're going home."

THIRTY ONE

"Bones? We're shipping out," Maddock called as he barreled down the stone stairs. The corpse of the sabertoothed tiger lay where it had fallen, the color from its pelt dulled in the dim emergency lighting. A thick pool of blood had spread out from its wounds as the beast's heart had pumped out the last of its life, reaching either side of the narrow passage. It didn't look as if the crazy Russian was playing ball. Bones had him up against the wall and was going through various makeshift torture-threats to try and loosen his lips, but the man continued to babble in unintelligible Russian. Bones had dragged him from room to room, looking frantically for the antidote in whatever shape or form it might take, but with no idea of what he was really looking for it was an impossible task the Russian was only too happy to make harder.

"We're screwed," Bones said. There was resignation in his voice, already at peace with his fate.

"Maybe not." Maddock said. "How long do you reckon it's been since our friend here shattered that egg?"

"Fifteen, maybe twenty minutes, tops. Why?"

"We should be dead by now if we'd breathed any of it in."

"How do you know?"

"Long story," Maddock said. "Let's just say we've got our hands on some insider knowledge. Time to move out. We're going home."

Sensing that their attention was elsewhere, the Russian made his move. He reached inside his coat.

Maddock acted on instinct.

Within the impossibly long second between heartbeats his hand reached for his weapon, his reactions so much better than the old man, even so it felt as if he were moving in slow motion. The Russian pulled his hand back out as Maddock released a single shot. A red dot bloomed in the middle of the man's forehead, snapping his head back. It never returned to its natural position. A silent cry died stillborn on his lips. With his eyes still open he slid to the ground.

He regretted it instantly. Dead men didn't talk. He'd never know what he'd been doing down here, how he'd brought an extinct species back, or even how many people had died at his hand here, guinea pigs for his mad experiments. The regret didn't last. Some sick souls deserved to die. It was as black and white as that.

He closed the distance to the dead man, bending over the corpse and pulling back his jacket.

He had expected to find the dead man's hand wrapped around a gun.

It wasn't.

His fist was clenched around a glass vial.

He pried it out of the dead man's grasp and held it up to the feeble light. Was this it? Was this the virus suspended in liquid form ready to be unleashed on the unsuspecting world?

Was that it, a suicidal Hail Mary distinctly lacking in grace?

There was no knowing what was going on inside the head of a fanatic, no matter what the cause.

THIRTY TWO

The Super Huey had already set down on the ice outside the compound when Maddock emerged from the building. As he ran toward it he could see that Leopov, Bones and the prisoner were already on board. The rotor blades continued to turn. Head down, he ran toward it.

"Where are Willis and Professor?" he asked, climbing aboard. He had to shout to be heard against the noise of the engine.

"They should be here any minute," Bones said. "They're just taking care of business," but the way he said it made the word sound more like *bidness*.

"They've got sixty seconds and we're out of here," said the pilot. "We've just had intel that the Russkies have scrambled a couple of MIGs and they're inbound. We are not sticking around for that. We need to be back out over international waters before they get here. As much as I love you guys, I'm not being held responsible for world war three."

"Roger that."

"There they are!" Leopov shouted, pointing at the two men as they rushed toward them. They ran as if the hounds of hell were at their backs.

"Go, go, go," Willis shouted, launching himself into the cabin. Professor was two steps behind him, and inside the chopper just as the runners left the ground. The wind from the rotors was fierce. The reason for their haste became obvious as they rose into the air. The main building was rocked by first one explosion then another. The backdraft engulfed the helicopter, sending it lurching through the sky as a gout of flame rose into the air. Another blast of air almost sent the chopper completely out of control. The pilot clung onto the cyclic and collective, fighting to keep the bird in the sky.

For a moment it felt as if he was fighting a losing battle as the ice reared up in the windows, showing them once again the bodies sprawled out across it, but he managed to keep it under control, barely.

The aircraft banked and turned.

Maddock could see the whole place was in flames.

In a matter of minutes what had been the Russian gulag would be consumed, leaving no trace of its evil past.

The chopper flew low, skimming the thermals close to the ice, churning up a snow storm as it headed back toward the ice floe and the waiting ship.

They saw the MIGs pass overhead. Only a few minutes after, they stood on the deck and watched as the missiles streaked down toward the ice, making absolutely sure that their secret was kept from the rest of the world.

It was closer than anyone would have liked.

His knew that his own government would never acknowledge their presence on the island, and there would be no funeral for the lost *Echo II* submariners, and no mention of the man they had liberated from his island prison or the biological terror he had created.

They might not be going home with Pandora's Egg, but they were bringing back the next best thing, the man who had made the contagion it contained. As far as he was concerned that meant the job was done.

His lone regret was that they had not all made it off the island.

ORACLE
A Jade Ihara Thriller

By David Wood and Sean Ellis

CHAPTER ONE
Teotihuacan, Mexico—Present Day

This is why *I love being an archaeologist,* thought Jade Ihara as she stared across *Calzada de los Meurtos*—the Avenue of the Dead—at the massive structure, known as the Pyramid of the Sun. Because she had spent so much of her professional career digging holes in the middle of nowhere, sifting dirt and, if she was lucky, finding a potsherd or two, she welcomed any chance to work a site like this, a place full of both history and mystery. It was a way of recharging her batteries. *Lord knows, I could use that right now.*

The invitation to join an ongoing investigation at the Pyramid of the Sun could not have come at a better time for her, both professionally and personally. It was a chance to get back to her roots, at least in terms of her career as an archaeologist specializing in Pre-Columbian American cultures.

Despite being one of the largest and most thoroughly studied sites on earth, very little was known about the origins of Teotihuacan and the people who had first lived there. Even the names given to the city and its monumental pyramids were the product of later inhabitants; Teotihuacan was a Nahuatl word that meant "City of the Gods" and was the name given the place by the Aztecs who discovered and occupied it half a millennium after it had been abandoned by its builders. No one knew where the Teotihuacanos had come from, why they had built massive pyramids—the Pyramid of the Sun was the third largest pyramid in the world—or why they had disappeared. The chance to solve that enduring mystery, or at the very least, shed some light on it, was one of the main reasons Jade had jumped at the chance to join the dig.

She strode across the broad north-south thoroughfare where Aztec priests had once paraded sacrificial victims before throngs of blood-thirsty citizens, and ascended to the Plaza del Sol, the courtyard that abutted the western edge of the pyramid. Up close, Jade could see the individual stones that comprised the pyramid. Unlike the pyramids of Egypt, these structures had been built with small irregular chunks of rock, sealed together with limestone mortar. Jade knew that, in its heyday, the pyramid had been coated with a limestone veneer and painted with the elaborate murals of feathered gods, priests and victorious warriors. The construction of the pyramids had been a massive undertaking, requiring centuries of focused cooperative effort, and had placed an extraordinary drain on the natural resources of the region. The deforestation of the surrounding landscape to fire limestone kilns was believed to be a major contributing factor to the decline of the city, but that was just one more theory that, while plausible, would never fully be proven.

"Dr. Ihara!"

Jade lowered her gaze from the pyramid to find a middle-aged man in khakis and a dress shirt, with a canvas duffel bag slung over one shoulder. She stepped forward and took his proffered hand. "You must be Dr. Acosta," she said.

Jorge Acosta, a professor of Pre-Columbian art history, presently serving as curator in residence at the on-site museum, was the project coordinator, and the man who had hired her on after a team member had been called away by a family emergency. The excavation at the Pyramid of the Sun was only one of many archaeological investigations going on in the ancient city, and it was Acosta's job to ensure that cultural sanctity of the site was preserved, and all relevant laws obeyed.

"Welcome to Teo, Dr. Ihara." His English was impeccable, without even a trace of an accent. "I imagine you're eager to get right to work."

"Please, call me Jade." His smile slipped a notch and Jade realized that she had committed a minor *faux pas*.

Smooth move, Jade, she thought. *Somebody loves his title. This is why I* hate *being an archaeologist.*

At least when digging holes in the middle of nowhere, she didn't have to deal with the fragile egos of academicians.

"I of course will continue to call you Dr. Acosta," she hastily added, smiling and doing her level best to keep her tone free of sarcasm.

Acosta diplomatically changed the subject. "We were quite fortunate that you were available on such short notice."

"Actually, I'm the one who got lucky. I just finished some work in Japan and was looking for…" She paused, not sure quite what she meant to say. Something different? Something to keep me busy? Something to take my mind off *him*? "A challenge."

"Japan? That's a rather strange place for an expert on Early American archaeology to be working."

"You're telling me," Jade muttered. Her work in Japan, specifically at the Yonaguni monument near Okinawa, had been a roller coaster of excitement—for which she had a healthy appetite—and drama—which was something she had lost her taste for. Her research had been pivotal in battling a threat from the international quasi-religious conspiracy known as the Dominion, ultimately making the difference in thwarting a Dominion plot to throw the world into chaos. Unfortunately, it had also meant working with her ex-boyfriend Dane Maddock, a former Navy SEAL and professional treasure hunter. Maddock had moved on with his life and that made working with him—working very closely with him— almost unendurable for Jade. She had made herself vulnerable, put her undiminished love for him out in the open, and he had ultimately refused her.

The rejection burned like an open wound, and the only way to get past it was to get away from anything that reminded her of Dane Maddock. It was time for *her* to get on with her life.

She sensed that Acosta was still waiting for an explanation. "The circumstances were unique. I speak the language fluently and I do have a background in Asian studies. Besides, no matter where you go, the principles of archaeology are the same, right?"

Acosta made a humming sound that could have indicated anything from disinterested agreement to mild disapproval. "Well, follow me and I'll introduce you to the team."

He turned and led her along the perimeter of the pyramid, to a dark opening that appeared to lead right into the heart of the massive structure. Jade was mildly surprised when, instead of heading into the passage, Acosta continued a few steps past the tunnel mouth and bent over a metal plate, flush with the sloping ground. The plate reminded Jade of the entrance to a basement, and she was not at all surprised when Acosta lifted the plate, revealing another opening that plunged straight down.

"I think I'd rather see what's behind door number one."

Acosta gave a polite chuckle. "That passage," he said, indicating the opening Jade had first spotted, "was dug by archaeologists. It doesn't really go anywhere. This shaft that we're using is the only passage we've discovered into the interior of the pyramid that was actually used by the Teotihuacanos." He paused. "Or at least that was the case until a few days ago."

"What do you mean by that?"

"You'll see." Acosta took a pair of hard hats and two flashlights from his duffel, and passed one of each to Jade. When they had both donned their helmets, Acosta stepped down into the opening and began descending a steep metal staircase into the darkness.

Jade followed closely, playing the beam of her light on the surrounding walls. After the initial descent, the slope of the passage eased, but the sense of confinement increased dramatically. The air was uncomfortably warm and stale.

"This was a lava tube," Acosta explained, his voice sounding muffled in the close quarters. "The builders removed the softer volcanic rock in order to reach the chamber under the center of the pyramid."

Jade noted that, while they were continuing to descend, the passage was snaking back and forth, following a course laid by natural forces millions of years previously. "Why?"

"I'm afraid we don't know that, any more than we know why they built the pyramid in the first place. The chamber probably represents the Underworld, but until we can learn more about the religious practices and cosmology of Teotihuacan, we're just guessing. Ah, here we are."

The passage abruptly widened and Jade saw that a small tent-like structure had been erected right in the middle of the path. The door was thrown back, and two people stood inside, hunched over a laptop computer.

Acosta tapped lightly on the side of the structure. "Drs. Sanchez and Dorion, may I introduce your new colleague, Dr. Ilhara?"

Jade quickly took stock of the two men that turned to greet her. One was short and stocky with a dark complexion and an infectious smile, the other average height and slender, with a mop of wavy brown hair framing a pale, studious face. The first man—presumably Sanchez—stepped forward quickly and began pumping Jade's hand. "Dr. Ilhara, so good to finally meet you. We've heard wonderful things."

Jade returned the smile, wondering exactly what "wonderful things" the man had heard, and who had said them. *Probably just being polite*, she decided. "Thank you. It's good to be here."

She realized that the other man—Dorion—was staring at her like she was royalty, or maybe a supermodel. "I've seen you before."

Jade noted the accent—*French*, she decided. *Not Paris, though. Somewhere in the countryside*—but it was the way he spoke, with an almost reverential awe, that made her suddenly feel very uncomfortable. Before she could respond, he added. "It was in a dream, I think."

Sanchez bellowed out laughter. "Paul is such a charmer. Watch out for him, Dr. Ilhara."

Jade didn't feel the least bit charmed. She glanced at Acosta, still feeling Dorion's scrutiny, then addressed Sanchez. "Please, call me Jade. It will save time."

"Jade it is. A lovely name. You know that jade was extremely precious to the early inhabitants of Mesoamerica. Oh, but look who I'm talking to. Of course you know that." He clapped his hands together. "I'm Noe. This is Paul."

"Dr. Dorion is our resident muon tomographer," explained Acosta. "He's the one who is making it possible for us to see through the walls of the pyramid."

"Muon tomographer?" Jade asked. She actually knew a little about the process, but decided it wouldn't hurt to hear it explained by an expert.

"Muons are high-speed elementary particles found in cosmic rays," explained Dorion. With the shift to his area of expertise, his voice lost some of its creepy undertone. "We are constantly bombarded by them on the surface, but they are unable to penetrate down here—one hundred meters underground. At least, this is the case where the pyramid is solid. Where there are gaps—tunnels and chambers—the muons can pass through and reach the detector."

"Like an X-ray machine?"

"Exactly. Only subatomic particles can penetrate much deeper than X-rays."

"It's working, too," added Sanchez. "Paul, show her what we've found."

Dorion stepped back inside the enclosure and bent over the computer, tapping out a few quick commands. The lines of text on the screen were replaced by a blue screen with blossoms of yellow and orange that reminded Jade of a Magic-Eye photo. Dorion continued to manipulate the image and Jade saw the largest blossom began moving vertically down the screen.

"What am I looking at here?"

"Particle frequency is abnormally high in the quadrant we've been monitoring."

Sanchez pointed into the chamber just past the enclosure. "There's a passage just behind that wall."

"We think there's a passage," amended Acosta.

"The data are consistent with there being a hollow space in the pyramid," Dorion said.

"But that's not the best part," Sanchez went on, with child-like enthusiasm. "Paul, show her the model."

Dorion tapped a few more keys and the blue screen vanished, replaced instead by a transparent three-dimensional representation of the pyramid. The chamber in which they now stood and the tunnel leading to it appeared as a pale red artery, ending in four-headed bulb directly below the apex, while a blue vein snaked a vertical course to a smaller cavity directly above them.

Sanchez pointed an eager finger at the picture. "The passage doesn't extend to the exterior. It's probably been sealed since the time of the pyramid's construction."

Jade grasped the reason for Sanchez's enthusiasm. A sealed chamber might offer an unprecedented glimpse into the origins of Teotihuacan and its inhabitants. "Why a vertical shaft going nowhere?"

"A sacred well?" Acosta speculated. "If this is a tomb, it might well represent a passage to the Underworld. Or it may be some part of the original inhabitants' belief system that we have never seen before. That's what we hope to learn when we explore the chamber."

"When can we enter the chamber?"

"We have to proceed carefully," Acosta went on. "We are dedicated to minimizing the impact to the site, but of course when word of this gets out, it will become very difficult to protect whatever treasures—in the archaeological sense—may lie within. Our plan is to dig a small intersecting shaft, just large enough to insert a robotic vehicle. I'd like you to take care of excavation, Dr. Ilhara, but remember, we only want to get a look at what's in there. We won't be taking anything out."

The restriction did not bother Jade in the slightest. She felt the group's excitement catch fire within her. Suddenly, even Dorion's strange manner seemed irrelevant. "Then let's get started."

This, she thought, *is why I love being an archaeologist.*

ABOUT THE AUTHORS

David Wood is the author of the popular action-adventure series, The Dane Maddock Adventures, as well as several stand-alone works and two series for young adults. Under his David Debord pen name he is the author of the Absent Gods fantasy series. When not writing, he co-hosts the Authorcast podcast. David and his family live in Santa Fe, New Mexico. Visit him online at www.davidwoodweb.com.

Steven Savile has written for Doctor Who, Torchwood, Primeval, Stargate, Warhammer, Slaine, Fireborn, Pathfinder, Arkham Horror, Risen, and other popular game and comic worlds. His novels have been published in eight languages to date, including the Italian bestseller L'eridita. He won the International Media Association of Tie-In Writers award for his Primeval novel, SHADOW OF THE JAGUAR, published by Titan, in 2010, and The inaugural Lifeboat to the Stars award for TAU CETI (co-authored with Kevin J. Anderson). SILVER, his debut thriller reached #2 in the Amazon UK e-charts in the summer of 2011. It was among the UK's top 30 bestselling novels of 2011 according to The Bookseller. The series continues in Solomon's Seal, WarGod, and Lucifer's Machine, and is available in a variety of languages. His latest books include HNIC (along with the legendary Hip Hop artist Prodigy, of Mobb Deep) which was Library Journal's Pick of the Month, the Lovecraftian horror, The Sign of Glaaki, co-written with Steve Lockley, and has recently started writing the popular Rogue Angel novels as Alex Archer. The first of which, Grendel's Curse, came out in May. He has lived in Sweden for the last 17 years.

CPSIA information can be obtained at www.ICGtesting.com
Printed in the USA
LVOW07s0028291014

410992LV00008B/1514/P